HERO
THE
GREYHOUND

by

Fiona Bennett

Grosvenor House
Publishing Limited

The right of Fiona Bennett to be identified as the author of this
work has been asserted in accordance with Section 78
of the Copyright, Designs and Patents Act 1988

The Hero illustration was drawn by Dominic Rae

This book is published by
Grosvenor House Publishing Ltd
28-30 High Street, Guildford, Surrey, GU1 3EL.
www.grosvenorhousepublishing.co.uk

A CIP record for this book
is available from the British Library

ISBN 978-1-78623-912-9

"With her special insight and an ear for the musicality of language, Fiona Bennett weaves the unconditional love of a mother for her autistic son and that son's unquestioning love for an unwanted greyhound into a heart-warming tale of rejection, acceptance and the ultimate triumph of love."

Ian Mucklejohn
And Then There Were Three/A Dad For All Seasons

"'Hero the Greyhound' is a tale of unconditional love. The love of a mother for her son, the love of a boy for a discarded dog and the love of a dog for its caregivers...you'll never see a greyhound in the same way after reading this gem!"

Raymond Le Blanc
What You Should Know About Autism Spectrum Disorders/Autism & Asperger's Syndrome in Layman's Terms

"Fiona Bennett's touching story of an unusual friendship between an injured greyhound and an autistic boy, and the bridges it builds between others, is written with sympathy, knowledge and humour."

Nia Williams
Birdcage/The Colour of Grass/The Pier Glass/ Persons Living or Dead

"I've smiled, I've laughed and I've shed a few tears whilst reading 'Hero the Greyhound'. I've also learned a lot about greyhounds and autism."

Norman D. Lock
Daily Mail '30 Second Challenge' series

Chapter One

"...and it's Severn's Soul at eighteen-to-one, coming up on the outside but no, here comes Molly Mandy at six-to-one, I think she's going to pip him to the post but where's the favourite, where's Handsome Hero? He's won six out of his last six races; it would be a great shame not to add a seventh trophy to his already impressive collection. Ah, here he comes, right around the outside, running like the wind, a streak of black and white lightning, running for all he's worth. But now, Severn's Soul has fallen back into fourth place, not surprising to most of us, he is a relative newcomer after all, but he has years ahead of him so we have high hopes he will be leading the pack before too long. He would do well to take a leaf out of Handsome Hero's book, just look at him go go GO. And it's looking quite good for Molly Mandy who's hot on Handsome Hero's tail so she may achieve second place but I do believe he's going to make it seven out of seven, I really do and YESSSS, he's done it, by Jove he has actually done it again. Handsome Hero is the hero of the hour and has won this, the most prestigious race in the greyhound racing calendar at two-to-one. His owners and trainer will be delighted with him, yet another stupendous run. Molly Mandy lost out by just one second but she comes

in, in second place with a very surprising third place win for the outsider, Black Jack at twenty-to-one..."

Handsome Hero was a champion racing greyhound. He was five years old, weighed 32 kilograms and when he was running at top speed, it was poetry in motion. "Aye, he's a chip off the old block and no mistake", his trainer would often say. Hero's parents were Super Swift Sally and Magical Marvin; all racing dogs have unusual names, there are so many of them, you couldn't just name them 'Flash' or 'Daisy' because things would just be too confusing for the commentators at the racetrack. Sally and Marvin were champions in their day but they had long since retired and had been re-homed as pets, by the Retired Greyhound Trust.

Hero's life consisted of sleeping, eating, training, being groomed and racing and other than the occasional trip to the vet or the 'bones and muscles man' (a sort of dog chiropractor) most days were the same. But there was one day each week which was different. Race Day. Hero knew instinctively when it was Race Day; he could just feel it, as soon as he opened his eyes. There was a different feel about the racing kennels on Race Day, people bustling here and there, lists being ticked and dogs being checked before being put into their cages and loaded onto the large vans they used to transport them to and from the kennels.

Once they reached the track, the dogs were all examined by a vet and weighed to make sure they hadn't gained or lost more than one kilogram since their last race. Their identification ear markings were checked and microchips scanned to make sure they tallied with their racing records and then, the dogs were rested for about an hour and a half before being given another vet check prior to racing. Hero knew when he was dressed in his special numbered race jacket, it was time for his kennel hand to walk him down and parade him past the people waiting to watch the race. The punters would search him out, pointing and whispering "Look, that's him" and "Isn't that Handsome Hero?", "Wow, he's amazing, just look at those muscles" and knowing he was the centre of attention really put a spring in his step. Then, the real excitement began and it was time to run, to really run, as fast as his amazingly strong, lithe legs could carry him. He loved racing, he loved that split second when the traps door opened and he could accelerate from nought to forty miles an hour in just a few strides.

Hero was one of six puppies whelped to Sally at the kennels, one snowy January morning. The pups had what was known as a 'good pedigree' and the trainers had high hopes for this litter but as soon as they were old enough to start training, it was clear Hero was a special dog. He won all the fun puppy races and was always first back to the kennels for his feed. He was a lovely natured dog too. One of his little sisters, Seaside Sue, wasn't as strong as the others so he would make room for her at the feeding stations and let her stand next to him so she got enough food and water. She often snuggled up to him at bedtime, he was definitely her hero and she was very attached to her big brother.

Training started in earnest when the pups were about fourteen months old and their bones and muscles had developed well enough for them to begin sprinting and chasing a lure. Hero may not have been the biggest in the litter but he was certainly the fastest and he continued to beat all his brothers and sisters during the training sessions. His little sister, Sue, was not as confident; she was not a natural runner. In fact, the first time they took her to the race track, she wouldn't come out of the traps, and she just stood inside, quivering in fear. The following day, Hero watched as Sue was taken from her enclosure and put into the back of a van. He barked to try and get her attention, she looked around, saw him watching and tried to wag her tail but she was so frightened, she just couldn't make it wag because it was so far between her back legs, it was almost touching her chest. Dogs which couldn't, or wouldn't, run, were no use to anyone. The whole point of a racing greyhound was for it to win races, to win money for its owners and trainers. Hero was frantic and he paced up and down, up and down, behind the wire fencing of his kennel but the van drove away with his little sister inside and he was powerless to do anything.

Greyhounds are usually paired with another dog in kennels and Hero's companion was a black female by the name of Wood Noddy (or Nods for short). They shared the same, long kennel enclosure with its concrete floor and raised bed box up against the back wall. Nods was an old hand, she was almost six and although she still won the odd race, she wasn't as fast as she used to be so Race Day didn't excite her in the same way it did Hero. She would hear the commotion, the bustle and the noise but instead of standing at the kennel door, wagging her tail and waiting to be taken out to the yard, she would snuggle down under the straw for just a few more minutes' shut eye and indulgently watch her younger kennel mate jumping up and down, itching to get to the race track.

Days turned into weeks, weeks into months, kennel life continued along its predictable course. The dogs ate, slept, trained and raced and although Hero missed his adoring little sister and her endlessly wagging tail, he got on well with Nods. On cold nights, they would snuggle up together in amongst the shredded paper in their box bed, giving each other extra body warmth, they had plenty to eat and life was good.

Chapter Two

"Simon Matthew Ellis."

"Yes, mum?"

"Get your body down these stairs please, time for dinner and don't forget to wash your stinky hands."

"Hey, I don't have stinky hands."

"I bet you do. Everyone knows boys are stinky and girls are perfect."

"Hey!"

"Don't you 'hey' me mister."

"I just did."

"Cheeky boy!"

Simon was 11 years old and had just started 'Big School'. The school wasn't actually much bigger than his primary school, there were a few more buildings and more people wandering around but it really wasn't that big but he had learned that adults liked calling it 'Big School' and it really wasn't worth an argument.

"Right then sweetie, guess who has a birthday coming up? Is it a) Father Christmas b) Rudolph the Red-nosed Reindeer or c) YOU?"

"Mum, you know it's me, why do you insist on giving me multiple choice answers all the time? It's boring."

"Aw, come on you old misery, I'm just having fun. Anyway, what do you want for your birthday? And before you say the words 'a dog', please don't, you know it's not possible."

"So, you ask me what I want for my birthday, knowing what I want more than anything in the whole wide world and THEN, you say 'Don't ask me for the thing you want more than anything in the whole wide world for your birthday'. What is the point in asking? You might as well just go and buy me another book about dinosaurs."

"But I thought you liked dinosaurs, I thought dinosaurs were a source of infinite interest to you, Mr. Junior Palaeontologist."

"Well, they are but I'm never going to be able to see one in the flesh or own one or take one for a walk or have it snuggle up on my duvet when I go to bed so please mum, purleeeeeez, pretty pretty please with a cherry on top."

"No, I'm sorry my darling, we can't, you know I'm allergic to dogs, they make me wheeze and they make me sneeze so it's not going to happen. Now come on, eat your dinner. I've made your favourite, mashed potato with tuna fish and broccoli."

"You always make me mashed potato with tuna fish and broccoli."

"Well, that's because you won't eat anything else and look, I've put the tuna fish and potato on the left-hand side of the plate and the broccoli on the right-hand side, just how you like it."

(sigh) "Thanks, mum."

Simon was a quirky boy. He didn't have any friends. He found it hard to keep a conversation going unless the other person knew lots about dinosaurs or train time-tables (and so far, nobody at 'Big School' seemed that interested in either). He found making eye contact diffi-cult and got really fed up being asked to stare at people in the eye when he was talking to them, didn't they know how hard that was for someone like him? He needed to look away so he could 'see' what they were saying. If he looked at someone when they were speak-ing, their mouth seemed to be wandering all over their face and when he was asked to repeat what had been said, he quite simply couldn't remember because he was being forced to look and listen at the same time. He wasn't being rude, he just couldn't do things in the same way as most of the other children at his school and sometimes, he felt very alone and left out. Having a dog would make his life so much more bearable, just one dog, just one single four-legged pal he could call his own. A friend who wouldn't mind listening to him talk endlessly about sauropods of the late Cretaceous period in China and Mongolia or the fastest route from London Paddington to Glasgow at the weekend. A friend who would be waiting at the front door for him, when he arrived home from school. A friend he could take for long walks through the woods. Just a friend who would accept him for who he was and love him unconditionally.

His mum was mean, she was mean and horrible, she was mean and horrible and unforgivable and nasty and yucky and ...well, actually, no, she wasn't. She was funny and helpful (especially with the Dreaded Homework) and she loved him to bits. Every night, as he lay under the duvet and Mum was folding up his uniform (which he invariably left lying on the bedroom floor) she would always ask "So, how much do I love you, Simon Matthew Ellis?" and he would always answer "More than the moon, the stars, the planets, the universe, the Milky Way and all the chocolates in Thorntons" and then she would lean over and kiss him on the top of his head saying "Correct! That is exactly how much I love you. Night night, sleep tight; see you in the morning, bright and cheerful."

Simon loved his mum; despite the fact her cooking was diabolical. Thankfully, he lived on a very limited diet, certain tastes and textures made his mouth feel funny and his teeth itch so he tended to stick to the same things which made life much easier for his culinarily challenged mother. Her best friend had bought her a sign in the January sales one year which said 'I Only

Have A Kitchen Because It Came With The House' and it took pride of place, right above the microwave. Mum was a vegetarian and she sometimes attempted to make herself some quite adventurous dishes, even though she made the same old mashed potato, tuna fish and broccoli for Simon every night. Her custard and gravy were the stuff of legend and he could hear her cheery voice, asking "One lump or two?" as she attempted to pour the hideous liquids out of the pan. He loved his mum very much. The only thing wrong with her was that she wouldn't let him have a dog. Oh well, there was a new book out about the Carcharodontosaurus available on Amazon, he would ask his mum to buy him that for his birthday instead. And there would definitely be chocolate cake. He loved chocolate cake, as long as it wasn't too rich and it was on its own in the middle of the plate with no ice cream or cream. He said a little prayer that it would be a shop bought cake and not homemade and then, he fell asleep.

Chapter Three

Hero was owned by a group of people who all worked together in the same office building. A syndicate, made up of six men who had all contributed equal amounts of money to buy their very own racing greyhound, in the hope he would make them pots of money.

"What a dog!" (the clink of champagne glasses filled the air)

"Yeah, what a guy!" (clink)

"Can't believe he's ours, he's amazing!" (clink)

"CHEERS!" they all shouted together (clink, clink, clink, clink, clink, clink).

"I own his tail..."

"Well, in that case, I must own his legs, all four of them, ha ha ha..."

"I don't care which bit I own, just so long as he keeps hurtling around that track and winning us loads of dosh. Right, who's having the fish and who's having the beef? Shall we order another bottle of Dom Perignon while we're at it? Might as well eh?"

The six men were eating out at the fanciest restaurant in town having once again, witnessed their very own Handsome Hero win his race at that evening's meeting. They drank the finest champagne and ordered the most expensive food on the menu and then, they ordered a big 'people carrier' style taxi to take them home because they were so squiffy by the time the meal ended.

"We Are The Champions My Friend..." sang Derek tunelessly.

"And we'll go on fighting 'til the end..." continued John, as he clambered to the rear of the seven seater car.

"Hey", slurred Bob "what'll we do when Hero's too old for all this racing malarkey and isn't winning races anymore?"

"Aw, that's ages off yet, mate" said Pete, who had had the most to drink and was looking a bit green around the gills. The taxi driver suggested Pete wait a few minutes before getting in, he didn't want him throwing up all over the middle seats again. He was always very polite to these men, they were great tippers and he stood to take home an extra fifty quid if they'd had a good win with their dog, which would win him some brownie points with his rather miserable wife.

"Yup" hiccupped Derek "he's got years ahead of him yet, that pooch will just go on and on, y'know, like that theme song from 'Titanic'."

"So, when he's old and grey and lame, which one of us will take him home and keep him as a pet then?" asked Jeff "I can't, the missus hates greyhounds, she says they're horrible looking, skinny creatures who'd put you off your dinner just looking at them."

"Aw, that's not nice" said Gareth, in his Rhondda accent "they're beeeeooooootiful creatures, the best, the most fabulous animals on the planet. Anyway, how much did we win tonight?"

"Enough to keep us in posh dinners for a while" said John "and that's all that matters, isn't it boyo?"

"Don't call me boyo" said Gareth "it's rayshist, raysh... oh you know what I mean."

Another win, another boozy dinner and the cause for celebration, namely Hero, had been taken back to the kennels by his trainer and given his favourite meal of kibble, fish and raw eggs. Then it was bedtime for the fastest dog in the land. He had worked hard this evening and had managed to knock another half a second off his fastest time. He climbed up onto the box bed and snuggled up to Nods before falling into a deep sleep.

The following morning, Hero climbed down from his bed and stretched his long body, curling his back upwards like a cat and then, he gave a huge shake, almost as though trying to rid his body of all its fur.

"Open her up. Oi! You two, Jimmy and Neville, c'mon, shift yourselves, we ain't got all day" shouted Jem, the head trainer.

Hero heard voices and the sound of the main gates opening. Nobody ever bothered to oil the hinges and they made the most dreadful noise as they were pulled open by the two youngest members of staff. A large white van drove into the yard and the gates were carefully closed again. Racing greyhounds were worth a lot of money and the first thing any new member of staff was taught was to lock the gates and to make sure none of the dogs could get out. Security at the kennels was tight. There were no signs to indicate this was a place where racing dogs were kept, just two huge anonymous green gates on a dusty side road off the main dual carriageway. The only people who knew what lay behind those gates were the people involved in the racing industry and that's the way they wanted it to remain.

Yelps of excitement came from the van. Hero was curious and stood as close to the front of his kennel as possible, straining his neck to see who was making such a din. The van doors were opened and inside were six cages, each containing a young dog or bitch. They were walked down the ramp, one at a time, tails wagging furiously. The head trainer paired them up, one male and one female and they were taken to their new kennels to settle in before their first training session the following morning.

Hero padded back to his bed and snuggled up to Nods. No dog could touch him, he was the fastest thing on four legs, the Champion of Champions and he had even been on TV. He was filmed walking gracefully around the paddock and being put into one of the traps. The rather vacuous TV presenter stood by the traps with a stopwatch "Ready, steady…GO!" she shouted and then giggled as Hero shot out and made for the first bend. He loved that first rush of adrenaline and the feel of the wind whistling past his ears and down his body.

"Ooh, he's really really fast, isn't he? (giggle) I could do with one like him at home (giggle), he'd certainly keep me fit wouldn't he?" (loud giggle). Hero flew over the finish line and was caught by one of the trainers who walked him slowly back towards the traps for his final close up. He was a star greyhound, no doubt about it. Articles appeared about him in all the racing journals discussing his diet, his weekly routine, his teeth and his grooming routine. In fact, it seemed people all over the country were mad about Handsome Hero; they couldn't get enough of him. He was in his prime and he was unbeatable.

'All good things must come to an end' so the saying goes and the following weekend, Hero's star fell from the skies. He dashed out of trap number five, made for the first bend, crashed into the dog in lane six and went head over heels in the dust. The other dogs carried on, number six managed to right himself (although the speed at which Hero had hit him had almost knocked him off his feet too) and the pack carried on as though nothing had happened. Hero, lying on his side, panting heavily, could hear the muffled sound of cheering as Danny Dan came in first, delighting those who had taken a punt on him knowing he was up against the fastest greyhound in the country. He struggled to stand up but he had badly damaged his back legs and couldn't bear the weight. The punters who had bet on him were worried about Hero but they were far more worried that they had lost money that night and would never again make a few quid by backing him in future races. Accidents were common and this kind of injury could mean the end of a dog's career.

"He'll be OK won't he?" asked Pete, ashen with worry. All six owners had abandoned their wives and girlfriends and dashed down from their VIP box to find their canine investment lying by the side of the track in a dreadful state. "Come on Hero", whispered Gareth, in his Welsh accent "stand up mun." He knelt by the side of the track and stroked Hero's beautiful, sleek head. Hero looked up at him, his eyes still wide with shock and fear. "What can you do for him?" he asked the vet "Surely there's somethin' you can do?" Gareth's Bond Street suit was covered in rusty coloured dust but he didn't care. He had become very attached to Hero and of the six owners, he was the only one who worried about what might happen to Hero when his racing career ended. The vet shook his head slowly. It wasn't looking good for Handsome Hero. In fact, it was looking pretty dreadful. Would he ever race again? Or even walk? Gareth looked up, still holding Hero's head in his hands. "Do you think we should...?" he started but then realised the other owners had vanished. He spotted them in the distance, heading towards the bar and in that split second, Gareth realised his fellow syndicate owners were walking away from Hero for good. He was nothing more than a money-making machine to them and now, the machine had broken, they didn't appear to give two hoots about the beautiful animal who was in so much pain.

He stroked Hero's head one last time, whispering "It's gonna' be fine, butty", before walking slowly back to his car. He had left him in the vet's capable hands and for now, that was the best place for the poor injured dog. Gareth knew his girlfriend would be livid if he didn't join her in the bar, he had promised to take her to a nightclub after the final race but he really wasn't in the mood now. She would yell and rant at him the following day but he knew she had enough money to get a taxi home and quite honestly, he couldn't face her or any of his so-called friends at this moment in time. All he could do was wait to hear from the vet and hope that things would look brighter in the morning.

Chapter Four

"Oi, you! Oi, squirt! Oi, SMELLIS! C'm'ere, I wanna talk to you. Oi, where joo fink you're goin'?"

Oh no! Simon had been spotted, despite keeping his head down and taking the long way around, past the music block and the school office. Jecko, the bully, had seen him and was walking towards him, surrounded by his cronies. A bunch of weak 'yes-men' who followed Jecko everywhere and laughed at all his pathetic jokes. Simon tried walking faster but it was too late, they caught up with him before he could get inside the school's dining hall door.

"What's wrong SMELLIS? Is you avoidin' me by any chance matey? Don't you like me or sumffink? Ha ha ha ha ..."

Jecko's sidekicks all fell about laughing as they formed a circle around him. Whenever he told his mum he was being bullied, she would say "Well, you must run and tell one of the teachers" but he was surrounded and there was no way he could get past any of them, he wasn't very tall and he certainly wasn't very tough.

"...erm, erm...no, I was just going in for lunch so if you don't mind..."

"Well, akchooally, I do mind, as it goes, I mind very much indeed because if I call you and you walk away from me, then I'm goin' to get very upset, isn't that right boys?"

(laughter from the sidekicks)

"Yeah, 'cuz I'm a sensitive little flower and I DON'T LIKE BEIN' IGNORED."

"...erm, erm...I'm sorry I ignored you but I really do have to get into lunch now because I have a piano lesson afterwards and I don't want to be late."

"Oh well then, if you're goin' to be late, don't let me stand in your way 'cuz we wouldn't want it said that we ruined your chance of becomin' a world famous pianoist, would we boys?"

(cackling from the sidekicks)

"...erm, it's not pianoist, it's pianist, I'm a pianist."

"Are you now? Well then boys; let us make way for the world famous pianist, Mr Simon Matthew Ellis Esquire, otherwise known as SMELLIS. Ha ha ha ha ha, c'mon boys, let's get out of 'ere."

"Thank goodness" Simon breathed to himself, Jecko must be in a good mood today. He scuttled past the sidekicks and made his way into the very noisy dining hall. He quickly put his ear plugs in and walked over to the buffet station, hoping they would have mashed potato and/or broccoli and/or tuna fish on today. He was already stressed; having to eat alien food would just be too much.

"Everything alright Simon?" asked his form teacher, smiling as though she hadn't a care in the world.

"Erm, yes, thank you Miss Burbage" he said, as he rummaged through the stack of trays, trying to find a rare dry one "fine thank you, absolutely fine."

He wasn't really fine. Lunchtime was a hideous torment, the endless chatter, the clinking of water glasses and the clatter of dirty cutlery being thrown into the buckets was enough to fry his brain. The ear plugs helped a bit and as he rarely spoke to, or had to listen to anyone talking, he needn't take them out until he had left the hall. It was strange, the sounds he made when he was playing the piano didn't bother him at all but the sharp sounds of the dining hall made him want to scream.

Simon's heartbeat had just about returned to normal after his encounter with Jecko. He had learned, long ago, that complaining about Jecko and his cronies didn't really work. He and Jecko would be summoned to the Head Teacher's room, Jecko would be forced to apologise, they would be made to shake hands, they would return to their respective classrooms and the following day, it would start all over again. It was just best to try and stay out of his way, which mostly meant eating lunch as quickly as possible without giving himself indigestion and then, lurking behind the science labs until the rest of the lunch hour was over. He had even created his own 'secret place', behind the school recycling bins and when it was all just too much, he just held his nose and hid there until lessons started.

Even the relative safety of the classroom posed problems for Simon. Those awful fluorescent lights were so mesmerising, he sometimes came out of lessons not having remembered a single thing the teacher had said. Once that hypnotic sound was in his head, he just couldn't concentrate on anything else and sometimes, completely missed the homework instructions which, sometimes, depending on the teacher, got him into a lot of trouble. His mum would have to ring the school and ask what he was meant to be doing and then, questions would be asked. "Why didn't Simon write it down like everyone else?" "Why wasn't he concentrating in class?" Blah, blah, blah.

Sensory overload was a real problem for Simon. If things were too loud (fireworks, aeroplane toilets, hand dryers), too bright (the lighting in the supermarket, the sun, the TV screen), too scratchy (woollen clothes and labels inside his collar), too lumpy (his mum's custard or gravy) or there was a single sound resonating in his head (the fluorescent light, a bumble bee's buzzing), he simply couldn't cope. He needed things to be the same, all the time, every day, the same foods, the same routes to school or the shops, the same TV programmes (with the brilliance setting turned way down low so it didn't hurt his eyes), the same bedtime routine. Same was good, same was safe and same made him more able to cope with life, most of the time.

The reason Jecko and his gang called him SMELLIS was because his mum had sewn name tapes into all his school clothes which read S M ELLIS. These were supposed to help him not lose all the different bits of his uniform. Unfortunately, Mum hadn't realised that, if you removed the spaces between the S and the M and the E, it read SMELLIS and on his first day at school, when Jecko had pinned him up against the gym wall, slowly unwound his scarf from around his neck and dragged it through a muddy puddle, Simon began to realise what a problem this was going to be.

"Oh ha ha ha ha, look fellas, our new little friend's name is SMELLIS! Oh, ha ha ha ha ha ha ha ..."

The sidekicks laughed and pointed at Simon "Ha, ha, ha, ha, SMELLIS, ha, ha, ha..." One of the sidekicks was laughing so much, he almost fell over. Jecko looked mightily pleased with himself. He wasn't a good reader so for him to have noticed that Simon's name tapes spelt this embarrassing word was nothing short of a miracle.

Simon was mortified and at that moment, he would quite cheerfully have put himself up for adoption because he was so angry with his mum. He had wandered into the lounge one evening, just before he started 'Big School', to find her doubled up over a mountain of sports socks, rugby jerseys, ties, stripy shirts and all the other paraphernalia that goes with the start of a new term, sewing like a fiend. She was wearing her half-moon reading glasses so she could actually see to thread the cotton through the tiny eye and she looked very busy indeed. Mum had had to buy all the uniform from the second-hand shop because to buy it new from the official school outfitters would have been just too much money. She worked part time so she could be at home when he arrived back from school each day and he knew, in his heart of hearts, that everything she did, she did for him so he couldn't bring himself to point out that the name tapes spelled SMELLIS, he just tried to pretend the problem didn't exist and hoped nobody at school would notice.

But they had noticed and he knew the problem would not just go away. Even if he begged his mum to change his name tapes, the damage had been done and Jecko and his gang would never let it go.

Between the bullying and not being allowed his own dog, Simon wondered whether life could get much worse.

Chapter Five

"Hero, Hero, c'mon boy, c'mon Hero, wake up, c'mon, attaboy, you can do it."

The room was spinning and Hero felt sick. He was just coming around from the anaesthetic; the vet needed to know exactly what damage had been sustained after his fall and in all honesty, he knew it wasn't looking good for poor Hero. He would need to word his report carefully, he knew the dog's owners would be devastated to hear that their money making venture was coming to an end and once, he'd actually had someone threaten to thump him if he couldn't 'fix' their damaged dog. One of the veterinary nurses came into the operating theatre and said a Mr Evans was on the phone, asking about Hero and should she ask him to call back? No, said the vet, that's fine, I'll take the call now, better to face up to things sooner rather than later.

"Hello Mr Evans, thank you for calling. Yes, I do understand you're very worried, yes, yes, of course, but if you could just hang on a minute, I'll try and explain. Hero has just come around from the anaesthetic and he's a little bit woozy at the moment but that should wear off in an hour or so. Yes, yes, I have the results of the x-rays but I'm afraid it's not looking good for poor old Hero. No, no, before you start getting angry with me, please believe me, I have done everything humanly possible to help him, yes, yes, I do understand how much money you paid for him, yes, of course, he was going to be your pension, it's all very difficult and very sad and I'm doing my best to explain..."

The vet struggled to keep Gareth Evans from self-combusting at the other end of the phone. Gareth had been appointed by the others, to call and find out how Hero was, after his op. He knew the others would want positive news and he also knew what happened to messengers bearing bad tidings so he quizzed poor Mr Howler until he was blue in the face but the answers remained the same. Yes, Hero had had a lucky escape. No, he wouldn't be walking anytime soon and no, he definitely wouldn't race again. Gareth slammed down the phone, sucked his teeth and braced himself to tell the others. He poured himself a large whisky for Dutch courage and started dialling Bob's number.

Having been bred from two champion racing dogs, Hero had been a very expensive investment and all six men had taken money from their savings to buy him from a top breeder. Their wives and girlfriends had questioned the sense in investing such a lot of money in a mere dog but when Hero started winning and their 'other halves' began showering them with fancy presents, holidays and new cars, they all agreed it had been a Very Good Investment. Now, they were just as angry as their significant others because their 'nice little earner' was so badly injured, he might not even walk again. The presents would stop arriving, the 'surprise' bouquets of flowers sent to their various places of work on a Monday morning (just to show everyone how well they were doing) would cease and who knew when they'd next get to go to the Costa Blanca for a fortnight in peak season? Owning a winning dog brought kudos and status but no more would they be able to brag 'Ooh, did I tell you, my Bob/Gareth/Derek/John/Pete/ Jeff's dog won again on Saturday? This is becoming a habit isn't it? Ooh, I wonder what he'll buy me next? He bought me a Cartier watch from his last winnings."

The six men, knowing they needed to make some important decisions, agreed to meet at the pub around the corner from their office, one Friday evening after work. There was an air of gloom hovering over the table by the window and they supped their drinks in silence for a while. Eventually Pete asked, in a quiet voice "Has anyone checked the insurance policy?" "Insurance policy?" spluttered Jeff, spitting beer all over the table "Insurance policy? You're being funny right? Nobody would be daft enough to insure a racing dog, too much like a bad bet, if you'll pardon the very bad pun. No, I'm afraid those money grabbing so-and-sos at the insurance companies were not remotely interested in insuring Hero. I rang them all when we first bought him but there was nothing doing." The irony of the phrase 'money grabbing' was lost on the others, they were distraught, this dog had cost them dearly and most had spent the winnings as they came in, never dreaming it would end so soon.

"Well" said Gareth, "we still need to pay for his upkeep, his food and the vet's bills so we had better work out how much we owe and split it six ways" "You are kidding me, right?" shouted Bob "my missus is so mad at me, she's moved into the spare room and won't even speak to me. I am not shelling out another penny on that miserable hound, he's let us down and now, we owe money rather than win it, how the heck did that happen?"

"But you can't just abandon us Bob" wailed Gareth "we're all in this together, we all 'ave responsibilities, to one another and to the dog, he've done 'is best, it wasn't 'is fault he crashed into that other dog, not really mun."

"Well, the stupid mutt should've been looking where he was going, shouldn't he?" muttered Bob as he downed the last of his pint, "I am not paying any more vet's bills, I am not contributing another penny to his physio fees and I am not going to spend one more minute worrying about that pathetic dog. That is my final word on the subject. Nobody can make us pay; they can't hold a gun to our heads and force us to write any more cheques and they can't stop us from just walking away. That greyhound charity won't let him starve, they'll cough up for food and kennel fees so I am now officially telling you all that I'm quitting while I'm behind. So now, if you'll excuse me, I'm going home to have dinner with my long-suffering wife. She was quite right, I should've listened to her at the start when she told me it would all end in tears." He gathered up his briefcase, coat and umbrella and stormed out of the pub door almost knocking over Gareth's girlfriend, Donna, who was coming to find him.

Donna Angharad Bronwen Thomas was from Gelli in the Rhondda valleys and she was in a right old temper. She had met Gareth Evans during a girls' night out at the race track. They were amazed to discover they had been born a few streets away from one another and so, to celebrate their Welshness, Gareth had bought a rather expensive bottle of champagne. They clinked glasses and he slurred "Cymru Am Byth" before trying to plant a kiss on her magenta pink lips. Donna avoided him (she didn't fancy him at all) and tried to distract him by asking what he did for a living. When he told her he worked in IT but was at the track because he co-owned the winning dog, she suddenly realised she was in love (with his wallet) and lunged forwards to give him a passionate kiss.

That was six months ago and today, the last thing on her mind was kissing Gareth Evans. "Oi, look where ewer goin', ew stewpid twit" she yelled at Bob who was doing his best to avoid her as he left the pub. Donna was dressed head-to-toe in Stella McCartney and was tottering dangerously on her six-inch heel Louboutins in the doorway of the pub.

"Oh no," said Gareth to himself but he stood up, trying very hard to smile and look happy to see her "Hiya luv, what are you doing year?" "Whar am I doin' year? WHAR AM I DOIN' YEAR? What the 'eck do you THINK I'm doin' year? I'm year because I am absoliwtly, tautally mortified at whar've just 'appened to me, THAT'S WHAT I'M DOIN' YEAR. 'Ow about yew? What are YEW doin' year, spendin' money WE 'AVEN'T GOT BECAUSE OF THAT STEWPID, USELESS DOG?!"

Her voice was getting louder and louder and higher and higher so a very embarrassed Gareth took her arm and tried to steer her towards the bar.

"Let me buy you a drink luv, that'll calm you down." Donna thumped him on the shoulder and screamed "GEROFF ME, YEW STEWPID TWIT! I've only been and gone an' 'ad my card refused, 'aven't I?" "What card's that then, luv?" he asked, his Welsh accent becoming more pronounced by the minute. It always did when Donna was going off on one.

The others were finishing their drinks, clearly wanting to get away from Gareth's hysterical and strangely orange coloured girlfriend. "The one 'EW GIVE ME, 'EW STEWPID STEWPID IDIOT, the one 'ew told me 'ad a credit limit of TWINTY THOUSAND QUID! Do you remember givin' me that card? Well, if 'ew do, then 'ew might be interested to year that I've just tried to pay for my weekly gel nail fillers an' spray tannin' session with it an' when I went to pay Scheherazade over by there at the till, SHE ONLY WENT AND TOLD ME THE CARD 'AVE BEEN REFIWSED!" She threw her Givenchy handbag at her long-suffering boyfriend and burst into tears. Derek, who was almost out of the pub door, turned to wave sympathetically at Gareth before heading home to his disgruntled wife, Zoe. She might be angry with him but at least she wouldn't embarrass him in public in this way (and she wasn't the colour of a Jaffa orange).

Donna drank the half of cider and blackcurrant Gareth had bought her and he continued trying to console her while the others left as quickly and as quietly as possible. Co-owning a champion racing greyhound had been a blast while the dog was winning every race he entered but now, the syndicate's backslapping 'bonhomie' was fading quick and fast.

The evening had ended on a sour note, none of the syndicate members was prepared to take the dog home as a pet and they didn't want to have to pay to keep him in kennels so, in a round robin e-mail sent by Bob the following day, he suggested they all keep a low profile, avoid any form of communication with the dog's trainer and kennels owner and if anyone asked who was in charge of the syndicate, they should just keep passing the buck to one another until people got fed up asking and just left them alone. They'd paid out enough for that dog and couldn't possibly be expected to fund his upkeep now he wasn't winning any more.

The following morning, the terrible truth hit Gareth like a tonne of bricks. Donna had packed her Louis Vuitton cases and gone to stay with her sister (making sure to take every piece of jewellery he had ever bought her) and he was left all alone. He put the kettle on, made himself a cuppa and sat, thinking and thinking. Who on earth was going to look after Hero now?

Chapter Six

"I can't eat it like that" whispered Simon

"Why not?" asked Muriel the Dinner Lady (there was only one Muriel at Simon's school but she was always known as Muriel the Dinner Lady) "and speak up sonny, I can't hear you."

"Because, well, erm...because..." Simon knew Jecko was lurking in the queue behind him, eavesdropping and trying to find even more reasons to tease and bully him in the playground so he leaned a little closer and tried to explain.

"It's because you've put the tuna fish with the broccoli instead of with the mashed potato and now, it's all mixed together which means I can't eat it, because it's all mixed together and, and..." Simon could feel one of his meltdowns brewing; he took a very deep breath and hoped he was making himself understood.

"Well, I never did! No, I never ever did, honest I didn't!" exclaimed Muriel the Dinner Lady "what on earth do you mean? What difference does it make where the tuna fish goes? I put this lovely, nourishing food on your plate and you eat it. Isn't that how it works?"

"Well, not quite", Simon's whisper was almost inaudible now. He could see that Jecko had moved up two places in the queue and was now standing right behind him, breathing his yucky breath down the back of Simon's neck.

"What's the matter Mrs Muriel?" asked Jecko "can I 'elp?" He knew he would find out more about Simon the Skinny Weirdo by joining in with this conversation and then, he would have even more ammo with which to taunt him after lunch.

"Well," said Muriel the Dinner Lady, in her most sainted voice "I try my best, really I do. I do my very utmost to please all you young people in this school, really I do. What with my varicose veins, my lumbago, my sciatica and my giddy spells, I'm a martyr to my own body and all I get is moaning, complaining and unreasonable requests. I mean, I ask you! What different does it make whether the mashed potato is mixed with the tuna fish or with the broccoli? It all goes down the same cakehole dunnit?"

"Yes, yes it does, Mrs Muriel", grinned Jecko, who now knew Simon was in a tizzy because his food had been mixed together on the plate.

"'Ere, Smellis, why don't I 'elp you with this?" he hissed, leaning forwards and pushing the tuna fish and broccoli towards the mashed potato with his fingers. Simon gulped; there was no way on earth he was going to be able to eat the food now that Jecko has touched it with his filthy dirty germ ridden digits. Simon's mum had informed the school office, when he started at St Bede's that Simon had certain 'requirements' which included having the scratchy labels cut out of any new uniform, not being able to sit near flickering fluorescent lights and only eating certain foods, placed on the plate in a particular way. Muriel the Dinner Lady, who had been off sick (with her varicose veins, her lumbago, her sciatica and her giddy spells) for the first few weeks of the autumn term, simply didn't understand any of this; she thought he was just being difficult and now, horror of horrors, Jecko knew he had a problem with the layout of the food on his plate and now, he could use this information to make his life even more difficult.

Simon's brain had paused the scene and although he could see Muriel the Dinner Lady and Jecko's faces and he could see their mouths moving, he couldn't hear anything because his brain had temporarily frozen, this sometimes happened when he was stressed. Suddenly, his brain decided to start working again and he tried to take control of the situation.

" 'Erm" he said "erm, I'm not actually feeling that hungry at the moment. I think I'll wait until I get home..." and before Jecko could grab his arm, he squeezed past him and legged it out of the dinner hall, over to his 'secret place', the place even Jecko and his friends hadn't yet discovered when they came looking for him. The cubby hole behind the school bins was a bit smelly, it was where they dumped all the lunchtime leftovers, into huge green wheelie bins ready to be taken to the local tip and today, it smelled much worse than usual because yesterday, there had been fish on the menu. Nondescript square fish in some sort of white gluey sauce which most of the children had put into the slops bin because it was so revolting. The bins were really ponging today but despite the horrible smell, the place was quiet and nobody would bother him there so he just sat on the wall, holding his nose and breathing through his mouth and waited for the after lunch lesson bell to ring.

Dingalingalingaling. The bell sounded and the children all trooped into their respective classrooms.

"Today, boys and girls, we are going to try an educational experiment" trilled Miss Landers who was the Head of Lower School. The children muttered and giggled and whispered to one another. What on earth could it be? Miss Landers continued in her rather high pitched, wobbly voice "We are going to borrow some pupils from Class 8 and bring them into Class 7 and vice versa. Does anyone know what vice versa means and from which language it stems?"

Miss Landers never passed up on an opportunity to teach them new things and one or two children put up their hands. "Yes, Joshua?" "Erm, does it have something to do with smoking Miss?" "Smoking! No, IT DOES NOT!" Miss Landers emphasised the IMPORTANT words in every sentence "what on EARTH made you think THAT, Joshua Jones?" "Well, my mum says her packet of twenty Woodbines a day is her only vice." "No, Joshua, it is NOTHING AT ALL to do with smoking cigarettes, NOTHING AT ALL."

Miss Landers was flustered and her voice was getting higher and higher. Luckily for Years 7 and 8, she had completely forgotten her original question and Josh winked over at Simon but Simon didn't wink back. Sometimes, he didn't understand jokes and humour, he liked to make up his own jokes. His mum laughed at them but other people didn't which was a bit disappointing because Mum obviously thought he was hilariously funny. Or perhaps she was just being kind. His mum was very kind, she would be so upset if she knew how miserable he was in school, how he dreaded every morning when the alarm went off and he knew he would have to face his arch enemy, Jecko, at the school gates. He wasn't always good at empathising with others but somehow, he could sense his mum had a lot of things to worry about. The cooking, the cleaning, helping him with his homework, her part-time job, paying the household bills (she always looked really worried when the bills came in). He wished he could make things easier for her but all he could do was try and hide how difficult his school life was and how miserable Jecko made him feel. If she'd known how bad it all was, she would have had to take yet another morning off work to come and speak to the Head Teacher and then, she wouldn't earn any money that day so paying the bills would be even more difficult. He felt it best to just try and deal with it all on his own. If only he had his own dog, he would have someone to talk to, someone to listen to him when he told them all about the dreaded bullies and how Mrs Moaning Muriel the Dinner Lady didn't understand why it was wrong to mix the tuna fish with the broccoli. Life was so unfair at times, why did his mother have to be allergic to dogs?

Miss Landers (having recovered her equilibrium after Joshua's unexpected question about Woodbines), announced which pupils would swap classes for the afternoon. Simon said a silent prayer *'Please don't let it be Jecko, please please please don't let it be Jecko. I'll eat mixed up broccoli and tuna fish forever but please don't let it be Jecko.'*

Miss Landers cleared her throat and said "Would those pupils whose names I call out, please remain in the Year 7 classroom for our double English lesson? (*'Please, please, please'* prayed Simon) and then she announced loudly "Susan JENKINS, Jonathan MORGAN, Achmed ALLIL, Emily THROGMORTON and Edmund JECKO."

Whaaaaaaat? Jecko, in HIS classroom? Doing the SAME lesson? Breathing the SAME air? What on earth had he done to deserve this? Oh well, at least he wouldn't have to sit next to him, he usually sat next to a silent, studious boy by the name of Louis. Louis didn't bother him and he didn't bother Louis, they just sat quietly next to each other and got on with their work. Miss Landers made her last high pitched and wobbliest announcement "Would those Year 7 pupils whose names I call out, please go to the Year 8 classroom for double maths? Alicia KELLY, Veronica MATHERS, Warren FLANAGAN, Denis DEMITRIOUS (*'No, no, no, please, please, please...'*) Simon was desperate (*'Please not...'*) "...and Louis MIDDLETON". Simon's jaw dropped open and he stood, like a statue, trying to piece together what had just happened. These brain freeze moments really were a nuisance.

Some of the children stood up, scraped back their chairs, gathered up their bags and pencil cases and walked quietly out of the room. Jecko was grinning like a Cheshire cat and had sneakily made his way to the back of the classroom, right next to Louis and Simon's double desk. Miss Landers said "Now then, those Year 8 pupils joining us for English, please make your way to one of the empty seats and get out your pencil cases." Jecko almost ran towards Simon's desk, pulled back the empty chair and plonked himself down. Simon couldn't even bring himself to look across at Jecko; he just stared out of the window, hoping the presence of the annoying Miss Landers might just be enough to dissuade him from even speaking to Simon during the very very long lesson. Jecko said, under his breath "Oi Smellis! Ain't this cosy eh? Just you and me togevver for a whole double lesson, as close as you like, right next door to each ovver" and he poked Simon in the ribs, just to show he had no intention of sitting quietly and getting on with his work. Oh no, this was too good an opportunity to miss. To be able to goad and tease the little squirt for a whole hour and a half was just the best thing ever. He hated English and this was going to make the unbearably long lesson more fun altogether.

Chapter Seven

Hero slowly hobbled from his box bed to the kennel door and pushed his long, pointy nose through the wire mesh fencing. He could hear the noise and bustle and he knew it was Race Day. He was on his own in the kennel; Nods had finally retired and the lucky thing had been adopted by a nice couple with two children. She was six and a half and although she was still quite nippy, she wasn't as fast as the new youngsters and hadn't won a race for some time. There had been much excitement the day they came to collect her.

"What shall we call her?" asked the dad "I can't stand in the park and shout 'Wood Noddy' can I? That would make me sound like a right ninny."

"How about 'Black Beauty'?" suggested the mum "I'm sure, once we've given her a good brush, her coat will shine and she'll be a proper beauty."

"Nah," said the dad "Black Beauty was a horse; that would just be confusing."

"I know!" said the daughter "how about Artemis? Wasn't she the Greek goddess of hunting or wild animals or something?"

"Ooh, get you," said her brother, digging her in the ribs "with your massive knowledge of all things Greek, you little swot"

"Daniel, don't be horrible to your sister," said the mum "at least she's learning something at that posh school."

"We could call her Artie or Missy, for short" said the daughter.

"How about Cleopatra?" said the dad "she was dark skinned and had black shiny hair, we could call her Cleo for short."

So, Cleopatra it was. They signed the adoption papers, promising not to sell or give their new pet to anyone else, made out a cheque to the Retired Greyhound Trust to cover the costs of the adoption and the dad lifted her up into the back of their enormous 4 x 4 before cheerily waving goodbye to Jenny, the volunteer who worked tirelessly trying to find homes for the many retired racers. She hoped things would go well, it could take time for a greyhound to learn how to become a domestic pet and too many people had returned their dogs recently, citing divorce, relocation to another part of the country or even allergies. Jenny knew that greyhounds made great pets for those people unfortunate enough to suffer from allergies. She had adopted a few out to people with asthma and never had any problems but only yesterday, she had had a man bring back his dog. His wife had left him and he was out at work all day so Jenny patiently filled in the return forms and sadly walked poor old Grey Gordon back to his kennel where his pal, Saucy Sandy, wagged her tail to see him again.

Hero watched as his own kennel pal walked away towards the family's car. She turned and looked at him, she'd never been a very demonstrative girl and a few people had said they thought she was 'boring' when they came to find their perfect pet. Nods wasn't boring, she was just typical of a racing dog who hadn't known much affection; Hero was going to miss her terribly. The kennel door opened and one of the kennel workers brought in an enormous blue female. Sunshine Sarah's name didn't really suit her, she was rather domineering and Hero thought she looked quite fierce. She sniffed around the enclosure, ambled over to the bed box and, totally ignoring him, settled down for a sleep. He already missed Nods, she had been gentle and friendly and always pleased to see him. Sarah, on the other hand, didn't like him one little bit and in the weeks to come, he would find out that she wasn't very patient either. His injuries had slowed him down and when he took too long to get down from the bed box, she would nip his rump to try and hurry him up. Hero soon learned to let her go first.

The noise from the yard was getting louder but he knew nobody would slip a collar over his head and walk him to the waiting van. His racing days were over and he felt so envious of all the youngsters trotting eagerly across the yard, barking and jumping up and down with excitement. Hero felt rather depressed and he wandered back to the box bed, knowing he had a long wait until evening when everyone would arrive back, exhausted, after giving it their all at the track. He listened to the van pull out of the yard, heard the brakes squeal as it reached the T-junction onto the main road and settled down for a nap, with one eye on the wire front of his kennel door, just in case any of the kennel hands had stayed behind and might take him for a gentle stroll through the fields at the back of the kennels yard.

Hang on a minute. Was he imagining things or was the kennel door open? He gingerly climbed down from the box bed and walked slowly and quietly towards the door. He was right, it was slightly ajar. He used his long nose to push it further open, the hinges squeaked, he stopped and held his breath. Nobody seemed to have heard the noise; nobody came so clearly all the kennel hands and trainers had gone to the track. He knew Big Ron would be in the office, he was rarely anywhere else and answering the phone was the most energetic thing he ever did but as it was Race Day, he would probably have had a huge lunch, put his feet up on the table, pulled his cap over his eyes and settled down for a snooze.

Hero made his way slowly across the yard towards the big wooden gates at the entrance to the kennels. It was nice to be out of his kennel, nice and a bit scary. The only time he was ever allowed out of his kennel was for training or to go to the track so just being out for no good reason felt a bit strange. There was still no sign of Big Ron, so Hero crept over to the office and poked his nose around the door. Ron was fast asleep, the sound of his snoring drowning out the noise coming from the racing channel on the tiny television they kept on top of the drinks fridge. Now what? Should he just go back to his cage for a long snooze?

Something told him that today was going to be a different kind of day so instead of going back to his comfy box bed, he wandered back over to the wooden gates. They were closed but because all the valuable racers had been taken to the track, they weren't locked. Hero nudged the handle, it moved a bit but dropped back down straight away once he let it go. He jumped up and pushed it harder with his nose. Ouch, that hurt his back legs but it worked, the handle stayed up and he used his body weight to push the gate wide open. And there it was; the big wide world outside the racing kennels. He had never seen it before; he had only ever left the yard in the back of a windowless van so the outside world was something of a mystery. Hero's back legs were still weak and sometimes quite painful but he was able to walk so he set off along the side of the road, occasionally breaking into a rather lopsided trot but thoroughly enjoying this new feeling of freedom.

"Ere, you, dog, whatsyourname? Oi, get back 'ere. Come back NOW!" roared Ron from the kennels' gate "you get back 'ere this instant, do you 'ear me? Oh 'eck, I'm going to be for the 'igh jump I am."

Ron had woken himself up with an extra loud snore. He blinked hard, stood up, yawned and stretched noisily and then wandered over to the office door. Something was wrong. The main gate was ajar. He waddled into the kennels area and seeing that Hero and Sarah's door was wide open, Ron ran as fast as his enormous frame would allow, over to the main gates. *"Puff, puff* Oi! You stupid animal, come back here NOW or I won't be held responsible for my actions, *puff, puff."*

Hero had heard the shouting and although he hadn't run for weeks on end, he decided today might be the day to see whether his legs would work again. His back legs felt odd and uncomfortable but it didn't hurt as much as he expected so he just kept on running until Ron was well out of sight. Ron had turned around and was rummaging in the office for the van keys. The ancient white van they used to take individual dogs to the 'muscle and bone man' or to the vet's if they needed more than just a jab or tablets. He found the keys and wobbled over to the tatty old vehicle. It took quite a feat of breathing in and holding in his tum to get behind the wheel but he eventually turned on the ignition and set off in search of the nuisance dog who'd escaped some fifteen minutes previously.

The nuisance dog was standing at the side of a very busy dual carriageway, wondering what to do next. Other than the race track or the exercise and training areas near the kennels, Hero had never seen a road and it really was very scary. What on earth was that? It looked like a human but not the kind Hero was used to. This one had wheels and the human was wearing something round, black and shiny on its head. 'NIIIAAAAAAAAA-OOOOOWWWWWWWW', the motorbike flew past Hero, causing his ears to flap in the breeze. He ducked away from the side of the road, the traffic was crazy. Cars, lorries, vans and the occasional motorbike drove past at speeds much faster than the race track vans. It was terrifying.

Hero waited for the gap in the traffic and ran for all he was worth, across to the central reservation. Cars beeped their horns and another motorbike swerved to avoid the flash of black and white fur running across the two lanes. His legs weren't really working properly and he was panting as he ducked under the barrier on the grassy bank in between the two carriageways. His tongue was hanging out of his mouth and his chest heaved up and down, up and down. Oh no, the traffic was coming at him from the other direction now and it seemed even faster than before. He waited and waited and suddenly, there was another gap so Hero took a deep breath and flew across the road, as fast as his poor old damaged legs would carry him.

He was thirsty and was tempted to go back, knowing there was a bowl of fresh water in his kennel but now he was out, he wanted to stay out so he just kept on running and limping, running and limping. Hero wandered further and further away from the kennels and the main road and eventually found himself in a field which was home to half a dozen scruffy old horses. There was a trough of dirty water in the corner of the field. He drank and drank, it tasted funny but at least it helped quench the thirst he had built up with all the running. He hadn't run at all since that fateful day at the track and now, he felt tired so although he was quite hungry, he decided to settle down for a rest, underneath one of the hedges which ran along the edge of the field. This was going to be quite an adventure for a dog who had only ever known the safety of the kennels and his weekly visits to the race track. Where would it take him next?

Chapter Eight

(Seven years previously)

"Autism spectrum disorder" said Simone Ellis, slowly, "autism spectrum disorder. What does that mean exactly?"

"Well, basically..." said the senior paediatrician

"No, not basically" muttered Simone

"I beg your pardon," said the senior paediatrician "what do you mean?"

"Basically is one of those non-words, those words people use when they are trying to buy themselves time, so they can formulate their sentences, it's lazy and unnecessary and it's banned in our house."

Simone knew she was being unreasonable and difficult but she was in shock. Dr Patricia Nolan, the senior paediatrician had just given her some life-shattering news and she couldn't bear to hear it start with 'basically' which was, indeed, a banned word in their house. She and her husband, Neil, would joke about it all the time. They both knew the word was perfectly acceptable, one of millions of perfectly acceptable words but then, someone, somewhere decided it made them sound intelligent, it made their sentences sound very important and suddenly, nobody seemed to be able to speak without using it as their opening gambit and everyone from newsreaders right through to the woman behind the counter in the local One Stop Shop was starting their sentences with "Well, basically..." so Simone and Neil decided they would ban the 'B' word from then on.

"Simone," said Neil, gently, "Simone, the doctor is just trying to tell us what she thinks is wrong with Simon, that's all."

"I know" she answered "but I can't bear to hear that word, not today of all days. I'm sorry, please carry on, that was rude of me."

"That's OK," said Dr Nolan "it's a hard thing to hear, I do know that and I promise I won't use the word 'basically' again if that helps. Simon has autism which means he has trouble empathising with others, his speech and language ability is badly delayed and he has trouble with social interaction, social communication and social imagination. This is a lot for you to take in right now so I'm going to give you some literature to take home with you. Read it when you're feeling a little calmer and then, we will contact you to arrange a second meeting where we can decide the best path for Simon. I hope that's OK."

Simone gave a watery smile and held Neil's hand tightly. "So, on a scale of one to one hundred, how bad is his autism?"

"Gosh, that's a large scale, I'm not sure..."

"Well, OK then, how about a scale of one to ten?"

Dr Nolan looked across at Sandra Dillon, the senior speech and language therapist, who had spent some of the diagnosis session with Simon and they both raised their eyebrows. "Well, about a three, maybe a four I suppose." Simone burst into tears. Dr Nolan had said Simon was almost halfway up her self-imposed autism scale and she couldn't bear it. The years leading up to this diagnosis had been spent worrying, thinking, asking, reading and wondering why her son didn't speak, why he stared out of the car window, smiling to himself, why he didn't respond to Thomas the Tank Engine or Bob the Builder in the same way other toddlers did? Why he ran around the house on tiptoes and why, instead of asking for a drink, he would grab her hand and drag her across to the fridge, jabbing at the door with his index finger? Now she knew for sure, her precious four year old son had autism.

A friend, who worked as a one-to-one support assistant for a severely autistic teenager, had given Simone some PECS (Picture Exchange Communication System) cards. They were small, laminated pictures, each had just one picture on it with a single word underneath so, for example, if the teenager (who had severe speech and language difficulties) wanted a drink, he would hand her the card with a picture of a cup or beaker on it and she would then give him what they had 'asked' for. She would look at him and say the single word 'drink' as she handed over the cup, in the hope that, one day, he might just repeat it back to her. Simone tried the cards but Simon just picked them all up at once, threw them up in the air, laughed as they all scattered like confetti all over the lounge carpet and then, went back to playing with his toy trains.

He loved his trains and would spend hours just pushing them along the tracks, one way, then the other. When Simone picked him up from nursery school, the girls would say in their sing-song voices "He's had a lovely day, playing with his trains." She was beginning to suspect they didn't really take much notice of him at all. They had a room full of demanding toddlers, some more demanding than others so, she supposed if Simon kept himself to himself and just played quietly with his trains, why would they bother with him at all? Simon had been a dream baby, quiet and undemanding and as time went on, Simone worried he might never speak at all.

She had been expecting a diagnosis of some sort but couldn't put her finger on what it might be. Neil wasn't at all worried but then again, he didn't spend much time with Simon. He was always at work and at the weekend, he spent most of his time reading the papers and watching football on the television. He had tried reading to his son and helping to build things with the building blocks but Simon just flicked through the picture book pages and then threw them across the room. Neil would build a castle with the blocks and Simon would wait until he had placed the last block on the top before smashing them to the ground. Neil despaired of his son. This wasn't how it was supposed to be, was it?

"Aren't you worried that he never speaks?" Simone asked her husband

"Oh, for goodness' sake woman, stop fussing, he'll be fine, just as soon as he finds his voice."

"But that's a part of it Neil, the autism I mean. If this is autism, it might explain why he doesn't speak."

"Nonsense," said her husband "I have at least two friends who didn't speak until they were five, they just didn't have anything much to say."

"But he doesn't do that toddler thing, you know, pointing to a dog and saying 'Bow wow' or 'Woof woof'. In fact, he doesn't point at anything when we're out together. It's as though he isn't connecting with the world at all." Simone wished her husband was as concerned as she was.

"Well, I think you're worrying over nothing, he's going to be fine. He's my son and he's going to be fine."

That was the beginning of the end of their marriage. Six months after Simon's diagnosis, Neil announced he was moving out.

"But where are you going?" asked Simone through her tears.

"I'm going to stay with Stan from the office until I find somewhere of my own," said Neil, feeling slightly ashamed that he was leaving his wife to cope with Simon and the dreaded autism. Simon was still silent and uncommunicative and Neil was running out of patience.

"Will you come and visit us? Will you come and see the local schools with me? I need to find the best school for Simon, please Neil, don't leave us. I need you."

"I need time to think," he said, sullenly.

"Well, it's OK for some then, isn't it?" shouted Simone as she followed him to the front door "How about me? I need time to think too but unfortunately, I have to look after our son and make sure he's OK before I can even worry about myself and the time I need to THINK."

She knew shouting at him wasn't going to help things. She had tried pleading, begging and asking nicely but nothing had worked. Neil couldn't cope with Simon and his autism. He couldn't even be bothered to come along on the courses which had helped Simone understand Simon's condition. It had been suggested he attend the Early Years Language Course and the Sensory Motor Skills Course but somehow, he was always too busy and just couldn't find the time. He had wanted a strapping lad, a strong, athletic boy he could be proud of. Someone he could watch play football from the muddy side lines on a Saturday afternoon, someone he could take to the pub when he was old enough. He wanted a textbook father/son relationship and what did he have instead? A four and a half year old who didn't speak, didn't look at him, didn't want to kick a ball around in the garden. Simon wasn't interested in anything much, just his trains. He was locked away inside his own world and so far, not even his mum had managed to break through and communicate with him so what hope did Neil have? He picked up his overnight bag and his car keys and without looking back, he walked out of the house.

Simone sat on the bottom step of the stairs and sobbed. She couldn't do this alone; she couldn't cope with her silent son by herself. Her parents lived hundreds of miles away and all her friends had young children of their own so although she knew they would be sympathetic, they wouldn't really be able to support her in the way Neil could, if only he had stayed.

She walked into the lounge. Bob the Builder was playing on the DVD, with the sound turned down. Simon was staring at the television, a puzzled frown on his face. He didn't look up when Simone entered the room; she had stopped expecting him to respond to her presence a long time ago. She sat beside him and put her arm around his shoulder, he shrugged it off without looking up at her. She felt very alone and very depressed. What did the world hold in store for her son? How would he cope if he never learned to speak or communicate with others? What would happen to him if something happened to her? Would his dad come to the rescue or had he left for good? So many questions and at that moment in time, Simon's mum just didn't have any answers.

Chapter Nine

The sound of a distant tractor engine woke Hero with a start. He had been asleep for hours. Escaping from the kennels and running all that way had worn him out. He was hungry and he was very thirsty but he wasn't sure what to do about finding food. He had never had to think about it before; he had been fed and watered every day when he had lived in kennels. He rose unsteadily to his feet, his legs felt like jelly, the injury at the track had really taken its toll, his back ached all the time and he still found it difficult to balance first thing in the morning. He gave a big stretch and yawned before wandering over to the filthy old trough. The water was green and slimy and he tentatively drank a few mouthfuls before deciding it wasn't worth it, it tasted absolutely disgusting. The sun was shining and the horses looked up from their grass munching to gaze at their new, rather strange, field companion. They knew he wasn't one of them but he didn't look like much of a threat so they just carried on eating and enjoying the sun on their backs. Hero walked across to the open gate, not quite sure where he was going or what to do next.

Then he heard a gunshot; he dashed through the gate and ran as fast as his damaged legs would allow, across three wide fields and into a wooded area. His chest heaved up and down and when he reached the woods, he turned and looked behind himself when he heard the first 'thud'. Something fell from the sky, 'bang, thud', another one, 'bang, thud', and another. What on earth were they? 'Bang, thud, bang, thud, bang, thud', three more of the strange round shapes fell and then, he saw several dogs, tails wagging, running towards the still, silent round shaped things on the ground. The dogs picked up the things and ran away, back towards the sound of the gunshots. Hero was scared, he hadn't heard gunshots before but something told him they were not good and that he should stay put, under the trees.

The things falling from the sky were pheasants. It was shooting season and the sky was filled with doomed birds, desperately trying to out fly the gunshots but failing miserably. They were bred and fattened especially for this time of year and the people brandishing the guns had paid a lot of money to be a part of this shoot. There would be lunch with champagne later and then, more shooting in the afternoon. Drunken shooters weren't the most accurate and the poor pheasants were often badly injured but still alive when the dogs rounded them up.

One yellow dog ran around and around in circles, sniffing the ground the whole time. Hero had seen the bird fall from the sky and knew exactly where it was. The Labrador, realising he wasn't going to find it, decided he should get back to his master before he got into trouble and ran off, leaving the bird in the middle of the field. Hero waited until the gunshots had stopped, it was almost lunchtime and there were fewer and fewer shots being heard. He waited and waited and when he had decided it was safe to venture out into the field, he quietly walked out of the woods and made a beeline for the thing. He didn't know whether it would be an edible thing but given that the other dogs had been so keen to find them, it was worth investigating. He would have eaten just about anything, so empty was his stomach and when he reached the middle of the field, he looked left and right and then, put his nose to the ground and started sniffing. Eventually, the scent hit his nostrils and he found his way to where the pheasant lay. It was dead so Hero grabbed it, running back to the woods as fast as he could. He ate the bird, chewing through feathers, flesh and bone without worrying what it was he was eating. It was food, that's all he needed to know and he really was starving; this was the first food he had eaten for two days and although it wasn't quite the same calibre as his kennel food, the meat tasted delicious. Now he needed a nice drink of fresh water but that meant returning the kennels and he wasn't going back there ever again.

The sun was still quite high and although it was autumn, it was an unseasonably warm day so he decided to settle down and have a nap after his unexpected lunch. He snoozed for an hour or so and then, the shooting started again so Hero decided to take a different path through the forest. He walked in the opposite direction from the way he had come in, through a densely wooded area, picking his way through the brambles and trying to avoid getting any thorns in his pads. Racing dogs weren't used to roads or forests; they raced on dirt tracks and found other surfaces quite uncomfortable.

He could see something shiny in the distance, in between the trees; something moving quickly in one direction. It wasn't like the other thing he'd had to run across, there weren't any cars or lorries here. He carefully made his way out of the woods and walked towards the shiny thing. It was water; flowing at quite a lick but it was fresh, clean water so he decided he needed to get down to it for a drink. The riverbank was much higher than the river itself and greyhounds find drinking from ground level difficult so this was almost impossible but he was so thirsty, there was no alternative, other than to bend his front legs as far as they would go and reach down towards the water with his long, pointy nose. He felt his left front paw sink into the mud and before he could right himself, he toppled head over heels into the water. The current was strong and his back legs were still very weak but the adrenaline was coursing through his veins, this was a real 'fight or flight' situation and Hero wasn't giving in. He was washed downstream and bang, he felt his left front leg hit a large rock beneath the surface. It really hurt but he carried on paddling for all he was worth. It wasn't really making any difference but when the only other option is drowning, you just keep trying and that's exactly what Hero did.

A man and his son were having a picnic on the riverbank. The son had finished eating and was throwing sticks into the fast flowing water.

"Hey Dad, Dad..." shouted the little boy "look at that, is it a dog?"

"What, in the water? I wouldn't have thought so", said the father, getting up off the picnic rug and running over to the side of the river.

"I'm sure it is Dad, he looks as though he's in trouble, what can we do to help?"

"Well, nothing much, son," said the dad "they do say it's best to let a dog make its own way out of dodgy situations, too many devoted dog owners have lost their lives trying to rescue their poochies."

"Can't we do something, Dad?" the little boy was desperate now, the dog had looked like a drowned rat as it sailed past, all legs flailing in the fast current.

"Well, I could ring the police I suppose," said the dad, fishing his mobile phone out of his breast pocket "Hello, is that the police? I know this may not count as an emergency, but we are having a picnic on the banks of the River Throng and we think we may have seen a dog in the water. Yes, a dog, it looked as though it was in a great deal of trouble, there was nothing we could do, he was gone before we could even think about what to do. We're about a mile and a half out of town so he's heading towards the bridge and the weir right now. My name? Yes, of course, it's Mr Jonathan Diddle. Thank you, I hope you can help him. If you send someone from town end, they might just catch him before he hits the weir. If he goes over there, I doubt he'll survive. OK, thanks, goodbye."

"Thanks, Dad" said the boy "I hope they find him, he looked really scared. Would you jump in and rescue me if I fell in?"

"Not likely" laughed the father and they made their way back to the picnic rug, hoping someone would find the dog and rescue him in time.

Hero was still fighting the current and he was in an absolute blind panic. It had rained quite a lot recently and the water was fast and furious, it was impossible to fight it. He was being washed down the river like a spider down a bath plug hole and all he could do was to take big breaths when the current allowed his head above the water. His leg really hurt where he'd hit it on the rock and he could feel his energy waning. Trying to keep his head above water was becoming impossible; his body went limp and then, Hero vanished beneath the surface of the fast flowing river.

Chapter Ten

"So, how's it going?" asked Nell, Simone's best friend.

"Oh, OK y'know, not bad at all."

"Come on, I know you of old, tell me the truth."

"Well, it's better than it was but it's still very difficult..." and with that, Simone burst into tears. Nell put the kettle on, made them both a nice cup of hot, sweet tea and sat down to listen to Simone tell her what it was really like to have a son on the autism spectrum and a husband who rarely made an appearance these days.

Things had actually been going quite well. Not brilliantly but quite well. Simone had decided to take her rather silent, introverted son out of nursery school each morning and in order to try and improve his communication skills, she had attended a couple of courses to help him with his speech and language and also his physical movements. She hadn't known a great deal about autism before Simon's diagnosis but she was learning quickly and with the aid of the SLT (Speech and Language Therapist) and OT (Occupational Therapist) sent into nursery to help support Simon, she was able to put things in place at home to help him too. Unfortunately, she was doing it all on her own, Neil still hadn't come home and sometimes, after Simon had gone to bed, she would collapse on the sofa, watch telly for a few minutes and fall asleep. Supporting a child with autism was tiring, supporting a child with autism on your own was exhausting.

"We're using visual timetables now," she told Nell, sipping from her teacup and preparing herself to explain all the new support systems in place to help her son.

"Visual timetables? What on earth are they when they're at home?" asked Nell, who had four year old twin boys and had never experienced anything other than the mayhem, noise and chaos of a normal pre-school household.

"Well, the Speech and Language Therapist told me that, because of his autism, he might respond better to pictures rather than speech, for now, y'know, it may not always be the case, he might be chattering nineteen to the dozen by the time he's five…" she tailed off, not really believing what she was saying "Basically…oh NO, I said it, that flippin' word, it's catching isn't it? She said that, for the time being, instead of bombarding him with questions or instructions, it might be best to show him what you want him to do in pictures and let him work it out for himself. Actually, it makes him feel very important, as though he's running the show but what he's really doing is following a set of instructions and turning over each picture as and when we've completed what it tells him to do"

"Right," said Nell "I'm really confused now. Are you saying you just show Simon a picture of something and he just does it?"

"Sort of" laughed Simone "although the pictures have to be nice and clear and he has to do everything in the same order every day, for now."

"That sounds rather like heaven" smiled Nell "silent children who do as you ask when you show them pictures."

Simone tried not to get upset; she loved Nell to bits, they had been pals for many years but if someone had offered her two noisy, untidy, boisterous children, she would have jumped at the chance. Watching her silent son play with his toy trains, never knowing what he was thinking, whether or not he was happy or unhappy, tore her apart and she would have given anything to see him join in with the mad games her friend's children played every day.

"And Neil?" There was a brief silence as Simone tried to decide what to tell her friend about her absent husband.

"Oh, he comes and goes, does what he can. You know how busy he is."

"Simone, sweetheart, you know as well as I do, he doesn't help you at all. He's always down The Lamb, boozing and playing pool and someone told me recently that he's..." she quickly broke off, horrified that she had almost blurted out that Neil was seeing someone else.

"He's what?" asked Simone with a real sense of foreboding

"Oh, take no notice of me, I'm so tired, looking after The Gruesome Twosome, I don't know what I'm saying half the time..."

"Nell, please, tell me what you were going to say. You're my best friend, if I can't trust you to keep me in the loop, there's no hope for me is there?"

"Simone, I'm so so sorry. Someone told me they had seen Neil down the pub a few times with whatshername, you know, that stylist from 'Fringe Benefits' on the High Street. Weird name. Really long. Scheherazing or something like that."

"Scheherazade? Do you mean Scheherazade? The one with the black extensions and the orange tan?"

"Oh God, what have I done? I'm so sorry, I really didn't want you to find out like this." Nell was really upset now; her poor friend had enough on her plate without hearing about her rubbish husband and his away-from-home antics.

"Well, I knew he must be seeing someone," said Simone, quietly "he hasn't been home for weeks now and even when I texted to tell him Simon was doing better, he didn't text back. Well, he did but it only said 'Great', nothing more than that."

She walked to the sink and stood, staring out onto the postage sized patch of grass they grandly called the garden. "Nell, please don't feel bad. You didn't make it happen, it just happened and I can't do much about it. Obviously, he's having a lot more fun these days. It's just sad he couldn't find a way to stay here and have fun with us. Mind you, most days here are not exactly what you'd call fun so I can hardly blame him for trying to escape, can I?"

"He's a cowardly scumbag and you know it" snarled Nell "he could have stayed, helped you, taken it in turns to do all the stuff you do with Simon every day. I have lost all respect for him and you won't thank me for it but I do think you're better off without him. Never knowing whether he would come home or stay out all night. You're a fantastic mum and Simon's doing brilliantly with your help. He is of no use to you at all."

Simone couldn't turn around to look at her friend because she was crying and she didn't want Nell to see. "Thanks love, you're a pal. I'll see you soon OK?" Nell knew she needed to go; she wanted to hug her friend but sensed she just needed some space and time alone so she quietly closed the front door as she left and started walking to the pre-school to collect her two. Most days, she hated the long walk to pick up her sons but today, she couldn't get there fast enough. "I'm so lucky, I'm so lucky" she chanted inside her head "Poor Simone, poor poor Simone, what the heck has she done to deserve all of this?"

Simone washed up the teacups and sat at the kitchen table. She picked up her phone and started a text to

Neil. "Hiya. Hope you're OK. Simon is doing well with his visual timetables. If you want to know more about it all, come and see us. We'd love to see you." She put the phone back on the table and stared at it. Nothing. No response. She knew he kept his phone in his pocket the whole time and she also knew he would have seen the text immediately.

The clock pinged five 'o clock and she wearily gathered up her handbag, checked her purse to see if she had enough money to buy Simon a treat on the way home from nursery, picked up her silent phone and walked to the front door. The door which used to fling wide open when Neil came home from work. He used to shout "Where's my favourite girl?" and she would shout back "I don't know. Will I do?" They went through this palaver every day but it had always made her smile. She would have given a great deal to hear his cheery voice shouting from the hallway these days but it had been a long time since he'd been home and in her heart of hearts, she knew he probably wouldn't be coming back.

She set off for the nursery school. The sun was shining, there were people everywhere; happy, smiling people, collecting their children from nursery and pre-school. Somehow, she managed to make her face smile as she approached the gates. Simon was waiting with his support assistant who began waving at Simone, hoping Simon would copy her. He didn't. He just stared at his mum. She took his hand, saying "Hello sweetie, have you had a good afternoon?" knowing there would be no response. Would there ever be a response? Would her son ever answer her questions, ask her a question, laugh out loud or give any indication that he was a happy little boy? She had no first clue what the future held but for now, she tried hard to keep her pecker up and to chat to Simon as they walked home, via the sweetie shop to buy a small bar of chocolate. Things could be worse; she wasn't sure how much worse but she had to tell herself this in order to keep going. *Why me? Why do I have an autistic son? Why not any of the other nursery mums? What did I do wrong? What have I done to deserve this?*

Simone chatted endlessly to her son, all the way home. He didn't utter a single word but he did make sure to walk only on the paving slabs and not on the lines or cracks; another of his obsessions. They got home and he opened the front door, making sure to shut it tightly again once they were both inside. Then, her rather obsessive son, climbed the stairs to his room where, she knew, he would be taking all his toy trains out of their boxes. She knew this because this is what he did every single day after school. Trains, tea, bath time, bedtime and then, they'd do the same thing all over again the next day.

"Come home Neil" she prayed *"Come home and help us. Come and make me laugh like you used to. I'll cook your favourite meal, I'll try not to burn it. I'll pour you a nice cold beer but please, please just come home to us."* And then, she fell asleep on the sofa in front of the Nine 'o Clock News.

Chapter Eleven

"I think he must have swallowed a lot of water," said a voice, coming from above Hero's head "or eaten something awful which has disagreed with him, or both. He's in a right old state, isn't he? Poor thing."

Hero was lying by the side of the river, wrapped in a thick blanket. He had been very sick. Whole pheasants are not usually a part of the average greyhound diet and the rich meat combined with the water he'd swallowed whilst being whooshed down the river, had made him feel quite ill. He couldn't see or hear properly, his eyes and ears were filled with dirty river water but he could hear a muffled voice somewhere above his head.

"That's my boy, well done. Come on, we'll have you right in no time flat" said the voice, rubbing Hero with the blanket, trying to warm him up. The voice belonged to Des, a keen fisherman who spent many hours sitting on the banks of the Throng, attempting to catch the odd fish and munching the corned beef and pickle sandwiches his wife, Maureen, had packed for him. He wasn't a very good fisherman (mainly because he spent most of the time chatting to anyone passing by) and often didn't catch a thing. He usually called into the fishmonger's on the High Street and bought a fish to take home to Maureen, just so she would think he'd caught something. Maureen was smart enough to know the fish was shop bought but also smart enough not to let on that she knew a freshly caught fish would still have a head, not to mention little dead, beady eyes. She duly served up the fish with chunky chips and a few garden peas and Des was none the wiser. He used his weekly fishing trip as a kind of therapy, to get some peace and quiet. It got him out from under Maureen's feet so she could get on with the housework and then, when she'd finished dusting and polishing their tiny little house, she'd settle down with a nice cup of coffee to watch 'Neighbours' on the telly. Oh yes, her husband's regular fishing trips were hugely therapeutic although she would pretend to complain whenever he collected his rod, net and bag from behind the front door. "You off fishing again?" she'd pretend to moan but he'd give her a wink, knowing she loved the peace and quiet, not to mention the drama of Neighbours. It made her humdrum life a little more exciting and it gave him the chance to sit and ponder and to talk to anyone who passed by his camping chair (with the cup holder for his flask) on the banks of the Throng.

"Where on earth do you think he's come from then?" Des asked Andy, the ambulance man who'd helped him fish Hero out of the river. The emergency services people hadn't known what to do when they received the call, telling them there was a dog being washed downstream towards Dorman's Weir so they decided the ambulance service was probably going to be the most helpful for when the poor creature was hooked out from the whirlpool below. Andy had grabbed Des's fishing rod and net and, leaning precariously towards the river, he reached as far as his arms would allow (Des hung onto him for grim death, arms wrapped tightly around his waist) and managed to hook the rod inside Hero's collar. He dragged with all his might and then, managed to get the net over the dog's head. Between them, they got Hero to the edge of the river and, grabbing two legs each, hauled him onto the bank. Despite being almost unconscious, Hero winced. His back legs were still very painful from the accident at the track and desperately swimming against the tide had really hurt his damaged muscles.

"Well, I'm not quite sure but I think there are racing kennels somewhere around here," said Andy "after all, there is a huge race track in town so it stands to reason that the kennels would be close by. I think they like to keep its location a secret though. These dogs are worth a fortune…well, they are when they're winning anyway" and he laughed loudly, sounding rather like a donkey braying. "Can't imagine this poor old thing winning many races, he's in a right old state. Look at that back leg, that's seen better days I'll warrant, it looks a bit twisted to me. What d'you reckon Des?"

Everyone knew Des who, since his retirement, had been a pretty permanent fixture along the riverbank. "It does, doesn't it?" said Des, studying Hero's legs with his eyes screwed up because he'd forgotten his glasses. "Perhaps he used to race, who knows? I'll tell you one thing though, those dogs do suffer some dreadful accidents at the race track. I went once, just for a laugh, with some of my mates from work. Did I tell you, I used to work as a Security Guard at that huge car plant, Gellard Motors?" "Erm, yes, I think you might have mentioned it once or twice" said Andy, who knew, if he allowed Des to start talking, he'd be late home for his tea and his missus would flip. It was the night she practised what she'd learned in her Jamie Oliver Cook Book Club and tonight, she was testing out her Three Cheese Soufflé with a Parmesan Crisp. He daren't be late or the soufflé would sink and she'd be upset.

"Oh yes" continued Des (feeling important because he knew about dog racing and clearly, Andy didn't) "those dogs flew out of the traps, like the very devil was after them and then, they hit that first bend and the one I'd bet on – I think he was called Handsome Horace or something like that – crashed into the one in the next lane, went head over heels and the next thing, the vet, the owners, the trainer were all at the side of the track in a right old panic. They took him away, the dog I mean, so who knows what happened to him? He used to win every race going that dog so I put a few quid on him but I lost a pretty penny that night; my missus was well annoyed when I told her. That might have bought us a nice meal out in the pub, know what I mean? This one looks a bit like him. Mind you, those big black greyhounds are much of a muchness, aren't they? They all look the same running around the track."

"Erm, yes" said Andy, wondering how to make his escape without appearing rude "Ooh, was that a text I heard land?" he said, reaching into his very deep pocket and fishing out a tiny phone, "I'd better check who it's from, I don't want to miss any important calls" and he busied himself, pressing lots of tiny buttons and pretending to check for messages. Des had never owned a mobile phone, he did not hold with mobile gadgets. What was the point in being able to escape the house if people could get hold of you at all times of the day and night? He could see Andy was busy so he turned his attention back to Hero, who was shivering so badly, his teeth were chattering. "Don't worry mate" said Des, kindly "We'll have you home in no time although, who knows where your home is, eh pal?" Andy had stopped pretending to listen to the pretend message on his phone so Des asked "Before you go home, could you use that gadget of yours to contact one of them, erm, animal sanctuaries? You know, the sort of place which takes in strays? What's that one that advertises on the telly, you know, they never put any healthy animals down, that sort of thing? Dogs something, erm, Dogs..Dogs...Dogs Trust, that's it!"

Andy used what he called his 'wandering Wi-Fi' to search Google and found a number for Dogs Trust. He rang the number but not before calling his wife, to explain that she might need to put the soufflé on hold, just for half an hour. About twenty minutes later, two people arrived and introduced themselves. One was the manager at the local Dogs Trust and the other was a vet. She opened up her bag, took out a stethoscope and kneeling down on the grass next to Hero, began listening to his heart.

"Not good" she muttered to the Dogs Trust boss "his heartbeat is very weak. I'd like to take him back to the practice if that's OK with you."

"Yeah, sure," said Jemma, who'd only been the Manager at the local Dogs Trust shelter for two months and had never had to deal with an almost dead greyhound before, "it's probably best. If he survives, we could possibly look at rehoming him but I can tell you now, greyhounds aren't the first dogs to fly off the shelves. People want cute, cuddly, lapdogs or chunky Labradors. They don't think of greyhounds as pets; they think they're too big and they believe they need masses of exercise every day. Ha! That's a laugh, my best friend fosters ex-racers and she says they are the laziest couch potatoes in the world."

"Right," said the vet "We need to try and lift him, gently, I don't know what other injuries he may have and I don't want to risk making things worse for the poor old lad. Could you two gentlemen help us?"

Des and Andy crouched as best they could and between the four of them, they managed to lift Hero up off the grass and carry him to the vet's van. There were plenty of blankets in the back and they gently manoeuvred him in. He let out a little cry as they lay him down. "Gosh," said the vet "he must be in a lot of pain; they are the most uncomplaining breed of dog on the planet, they never moan about anything. If he's making a noise, you can be sure he's really feeling sore." She placed two more blankets on top of Hero's shivering body and closed the double doors.

"I'll give you a ring later," she said to Jemma "to let you know whether he's going to be OK."

"Great, thanks," said Jemma "he's a beautiful dog, underneath it all and he seems very gentle. Some dogs would try and bite anyone hurting them but it's as though he knows we're trying to help him. I might even adopt him myself, if he survives. Fingers crossed eh?"

Des packed up his fishing gear and Andy bade everyone farewell before heading off home for his Three Cheese Soufflé with a Parmesan Crisp and a nice glass of red. He was starving, it had been a stressful afternoon and he was really looking forward to putting his feet up in front of the telly. The vet drove her van very slowly and steadily back to the practice. She put her phone on loudspeaker and called a colleague. "Viv, I need a hand. Just had a very strange call out to rescue a greyhound... yes, a greyhound, and he's a big one too. He's clearly suffering from old injuries but the worst part is that he nearly drowned this afternoon...yes, we just got him out in time. Can you pop into the practice in about twenty minutes? I should be back by then. I don't want to risk hurting him and I need another pair of hands to get him into the operating theatre. OK. Great. See you then. 'Bye."

She could hear Hero whimpering in the back of the van so she put her foot down on the dual carriageway. Her best friend and colleague, Viv, was waiting in the car park at the surgery. She smiled to herself. Viv could tell how much she wanted to help this dog and had made an extra special effort to get there early. They greeted one another as Jemma opened up the van doors. "Oooh, he's a real beauty isn't he?" exclaimed Viv "how on earth did such a fantastic animal end up in the river? Someone's head will roll when they find out he's gone. Right, here goes. Come on boy, that's it, gently,

gently..." and they lifted Hero onto the trolley she had already brought out from the operating theatre. They slowly wheeled him into the building and took him to theatre to see exactly what the damage was. Hero's eyes were closing, he barely had the strength to keep them open. "We'd better be quick," said Viv "at this rate, he may not last much longer and I really want to be able to trace his owners to find out what on earth happened to him and how he came to be in the river. Come on boy, just another few minutes and we'll have you inside." Hero opened his eyes for a split second; he could hear the friendly voice and somehow, knew he was being taken care of. "Right," said the vet, as they lifted him gently onto the operating table, "let's have a look at you, you handsome boy." By now, he was slipping in and out of consciousness and they both knew they didn't have long if they were to save Hero's life.

Chapter Twelve

"Good morning my little pumpkin" Simone whispered as she crept into Simon's room, "where's my favourite boy?" He opened his eyes and give a smile at the sound of his mum's voice and then, clambered out of bed and walked straight over to the colourful picture timetable stuck to his wardrobe door. The first section was called 'Simon Gets Up' and his mum had stuck some photos of Simon getting dressed onto the large piece of paper. He would check each photo and then, copy what he saw. Things had improved a great deal since the Occupational Therapist and Speech and Language Therapist had shown Simone how to make it easier for Simon to communicate with her and she really felt they were getting somewhere. They certainly smiled a lot more and that had to be a good thing.

"The lady who comes into nursery on a Tuesday is what's called an Occupational Therapist", explained Simone to Nell, who had popped over for a natter.

"Golly, that sounds important" laughed Nell "I wonder what it is she actually does?"

"Well, I've Googled it and it seems they help people with their motor skills, moving and that sort of thing.

If someone's had a stroke, one of these therapists can help them regain some of the movements they used to be able to do without thinking"

"So, how does that help Simon?" asked an even more puzzled Nell

"Well, she has suggested a few things. Apart from the visual timetables in school and at home, she's said it would be better if he sat towards the front of the class so there are fewer distractions. Y'know, the other children moving around, the big posters on the wall and that awful fluorescent light in the centre of the ceiling. He is easily distracted by sound or bright light and taking these distractions away is really helping him to focus more."

"Well, that's great" smiled Nell, glad to see her favourite pal looking so much more relaxed, "What else has she recommended?"

"Oh, loads of stuff, too much to bore you with now. Let's have another cuppa and you can tell me how your two cherubs are doing."

The suggestions from the OT and SLT had changed Simone's life. In the early days, Simon would 'get lost' inside his clothes. He simply couldn't feel where his head was in relation to the neck hole of his jumper and it had taken a long time for him to learn how to dress himself. The first time it happened, his cheeky face popped up through the neck hole and Simone planted a big kiss on his forehead. He didn't really like being touched but she couldn't resist him. He was coming on in leaps and bounds and she had learned too, that patience was a real virtue when dealing with her uncommunicative son. "What do we have in the Magic Fridge today then?" she'd ask, every single morning brought the same routine and the same questions. "Oooh, now then, I can see some of your favourite juice and the milk is lovely and chilled too." Simon really was a creature of habit and would only eat his favourite chocolate rice crisps with freezing cold milk. If the milk wasn't icy cold, he wouldn't eat the cereal. Still, saying the same things every day seemed to help them both; he liked repetition and he liked knowing what was coming next. Instead of dragging his mum towards the fridge and pointing at the picture of a bowl of cereal, he would say "Crithps, crithps, crithps" over and over, until Simone plonked the cereal in front of him at the dining table.

Neil had kept his distance. He texted once a week, asking 'How are things?' but Simone knew it was a hollow query, one sent out of duty and guilt rather than the intention of helping her with their son. Another friend had told her that he was often to be seen in The Lamb, enjoying a pint and a game of pool with his friends. She had been good at pool and she felt sad that he no longer included her in his social life. He hadn't been back to see Simon once, not once. Simone, who always tried to see the good in people, tried to understand and all she could think was that Neil simply couldn't cope. He didn't know anything about autism and the fact his son had been diagnosed with the dreaded 'A word' just scared him witless. It was best he avoided his wife and son completely; he just didn't know what to say or what to do and not thinking about them was the only way he could cope.

"Mama, mama, mama, mama, mama..." badgered Simon.

"Yes, sweetie?" responded his mum.

"Bouncy, bouncy, bouncy, bouncy, bouncy, bouncy, bouncy..."

"Ah, yes, good idea sweetie. Bouncy next." Take his word and add another after it. Good advice from the speech therapist. This would eventually enhance his vocabulary and who knows, maybe one day, they might even have a whole conversation?

There was a small, second-hand trampoline in the garden. It was quite old but Simone had asked her neighbour, Gerry, to make sure it was safe. He recommended putting up the additional safety netting. "Don't want you falling off and banging your head, do we?" he laughed "Don't want you having any sense knocked into you eh?" Gerry thought he was funny. Simone didn't but he did help her out whenever things went wrong and in the absence of her husband, his handyman skills were useful. He had asked her out for a drink but quite frankly, she would rather have stuck pins in between her toes and so far, she'd managed to find a reasonable excuse every time he had asked.

Simone and Simon used the trampoline every day (weather permitting). The OT had said it would help his brain but for the life of her, Simone couldn't remember why. She just made sure that Simon bounced most days and if nothing else, it helped tire him out and he slept much better at night-time. She'd learned to place heavier bedding on his body at bedtime too; he had been sleeping so much better with the blankets rather than the lightweight duvet. Something else the OT had taught her. What a miracle worker that woman was.

They clambered up onto the trampoline. "Pengwims, pengwims, pengwims" shouted Simon and his mum laughed and responded "OK then, Penguins it is." They played Mummy and Baby Penguin every day and she chased him around the trampoline, making daft penguin noises until they both fell over, out of puff but laughing like drains. Simone no longer burdened her son with long, wordy sentences, there wasn't much point because he didn't have a large vocabulary. She had been taught to say his name at the beginning of any question or instruction, in order to attract his attention and then, to speak in short, sharp sentences. So, instead of "Oooh, isn't it a lovely day sweetie; shall we put on our wellies and go out into the garden and play?" Simone would say "Simon (pause), wellies, now". Initially, she felt rather as though she was giving a dog a command but surprisingly, Simon really seemed to respond well to this succinct way of speaking and was far more likely to do as she asked than when she had blathered on for a minute or two.

Simon continued to attend nursery in the afternoons. The nursery manager suggested they come in after lunch as a new arrival often unsettled the other children and then, the commotion would begin and that, in turn, would upset Simon. They lived a short walk from the nursery school and so, after a light lunch of cheese triangles and carrot sticks, washed down with icy cold water, they would put on their coats and walk the short distance to the imposing red brick building with the gaily decorated front door. Once upon a time, Simon would absolutely howl when she left him at nursery and the girls would advise she made a run for it while they calmed him down. These days, she would take him over to the play area where the girls had put out his favourite trains and dinosaur toys and he would sit down and start playing with them. He didn't look up or wave, not even when Simone said "Bye bye sweetie, see you later", he just stared down at the toys and began his play routine. Simon liked routine and if that's what it took to make him happy and relaxed, then it wasn't much to ask. At least he didn't howl crying when she left these days and that was something she never thought would happen.

Simone walked slowly home, made herself a cup of tea and had a long hard think about what do to with her life. Clearly, Neil, although he seemed to care a bit, was in no great hurry to come home and so, maybe she needed to try and imagine a life without him. Just Simone and Simon, sticking to their routines, eating the same food and drinking the same drinks. It didn't sound like a whole lot of fun but it was a lot better than it had been of late. At least she and her son were finally communicating with one another, albeit in two or three word sentences and plastic pictures stuck to the fridge door.

Chapter Thirteen

"Well, he's not going to win any races any time soon but at least he's out of the woods." Sue, the vet, was balancing her mobile phone under her chin and making a cup of tea at the same time.

"What's that? You're breaking up. Did you say you thought he could win races again?" asked Jemma, the Dogs Trust manager, "We might need to contact the Retired Greyhound Trust in that case, they might be able to trace his owners."

"No, I did NOT say that" said Sue, "I SAID he would definitely NOT be winning any races again. He may not even be able to walk properly although if we could get him some physiotherapy, that might help."

"So, what would you like me to do?" asked Jemma. She had hoped to adopt the greyhound herself although her job was pretty full on and he would need plenty of TLC if he were to get well.

Well, let me see about some hydrotherapy, something gentle to help him build up some muscle mass again. Whatever's happened to him in the past, he has sustained some dreadful injuries and that swim down the river didn't help. I'll call you when I know what's happening."

"OK," said Jemma and set about her day's work of trying to home as many dogs as possible. Dogs Trust never puts down a healthy animal which means finding lots and lots of people to adopt dozens and dozens of pooches. They had re-homed a greyhound some months previously, she had named him Saracen. He was a big, brindle boy who'd been found wandering the streets of Portsmouth. Clearly, his racing days were over and whoever owned him didn't think it was worth trying to find him a good home so had just abandoned him on the outskirts of the city. One of his ears was badly damaged, someone had obviously tried to cut out his identification tattoo and he was very thin. They kept him in a pen on his own, he was (understandably) very nervous of humans and they hadn't held out much hope of anyone adopting him.

"What's that big one" asked Fiona, one of the volunteer dog walkers, on the first day she'd arrived to help.

"Oh, that's Saracen, he's a greyhound," said Nancy, a member of the Dogs Trust centre staff, "He's been here for almost two years now. Greyhounds are not usually people's first choice when they come and visit. He's a lovely boy but a bit nervous and of course, his chase instinct is strong and he's not good around small dogs."

"He looks a bit pathetic in his winter coat, doesn't he? Maybe I'll take him for a walk first."

Saracen was wearing an old grey blanket and someone had sewn two old school ties together to make a belt, they were tied under his tummy. It was not a good look for such an elegant hound. "Whatever you do" warned Nancy "do not take off his muzzle as you walk through the yard, if he passes a Yorkie or something similar, he might just think it's a rabbit and you might find yourself minus an arm."

Fiona had fallen head over heels in love with Saracen and a few weeks later, having signed the adoption papers and made a donation to the Dogs Trust, she took him home permanently. Jemma was a bit worried; the greyhound is a rare breed. Gentle by nature and yet, when they see something running, their hunting instinct is so powerful, they just run and sometimes can't stop so they need to be kept on a lead in wooded areas in case they run into a tree and knock themselves out. They also need to be socialised carefully and to get used to living in a house, walking up and down stairs, traffic, family life and all the other things they never encounter when they're racing. Fiona called a few months after the adoption to say Saracen had settled well and she was delighted she'd chosen him.

Jemma hoped the injured black greyhound would find his 'furever' home although, with his damaged legs, he wasn't the most enticing pet. Still, she had plenty of other dogs to re-home so she picked up the phone to place the weekly advert in the local paper and tried not to worry too much about him although she couldn't help wondering who'd owned him and whether or not they gave two hoots about him or had even noticed he'd gone missing. Honestly, sometimes the human race was so disappointingly uncaring; she much preferred the fluffy, four-legged residents at Dogs Trust.

One of Hero's former owners did, indeed, give two hoots about his whereabouts. Gareth's life had pretty much fallen apart after Hero's accident and he felt very down in the dumps. Donna had left him; now his wallet wasn't bulging at the seams, he held little interest for her and she ran off with someone who had a part share in a racehorse. He often saw her around town, driving her little gold two-seater, convertible sports car. If she recognised him, she didn't let on and in some ways, although he missed her chirpy voice and her ability to drink him under the table, he did wonder whether her shallowness would eventually have been the death of their relationship. She hadn't cared a jot about Hero. "That stewpid mutt" she would call him, in her strong Welsh accent; half joking, whole in earnest and when she'd heard he would never race again, that was the end of her interest in greyhound racing and even worse, the end of her interest in the slightly balding bloke who owned a part share in an injured hound. She was off to pastures new, making very sure to keep all the jewellery, clothes and posh handbags he'd bought her from his winnings.

'Where was Hero now?' he wondered to himself as he tried to decide whether or not to go to the pub. It wasn't the same these days; even if he did bump into any of his old race track friends, there was such an air of embarrassment, it really made him very uncomfortable. He had left his job, he couldn't bear to witness their total indifference to what had happened that night at the race track. None of them had cared enough about Hero to ring the vet and ask about his injuries; Gareth had begun to wonder what he'd seen in any of them and he didn't exactly feel happy about himself. Was he really like them? He hoped not. He'd been caught up in the excitement of owning a winning dog but had soon seen how things could change once the winning lifestyle ended. Like rats deserting a sinking ship, both his girlfriend and his so called 'mates' had shown their true colours and they were not pretty.

He hoped Hero had recovered well enough to be re-homed but hadn't had the courage to ring the vet a second time. Once he'd passed on the message to the others, that Hero might not walk again, they had all avoided taking calls from the vet or from the kennels. Eventually, it was clear the six work colleagues were not going to support Hero's recovery and the Retired Greyhound Trust had had to step in and pay for his food and keep.

He decided against going to the pub and switched on the telly. He half-heartedly flicked through the sports channels; football, horse racing, greyhound racing... wait a minute, greyhound racing. He sat down and watched the race. The dogs were simply breath-taking; they so clearly loved to run, it was just a tragedy that so many races ended in injury for one or more of the dogs. He paused the race and picked up his mobile phone.

"Hello, do you have a number for any dogs' homes, y'know, dog shelters, places where they might have dogs who need to be re-homed, that kind of thing?" The voice on the other end of the phone gave him two phone numbers, he carefully wrote them down and decided that he would stop feeling sorry for himself and would set out to try and find Hero. The dog had worked his four white socks off to win those races and he really wanted to know whether he was OK.

Chapter Fourteen

"And the award for the end of term General Knowledge Competition goes to...could we have a drum roll please?" Mrs Baker smiled at her excitable students, knowing they were dying to find out who had won the end of term GK quiz. The students began patting their thighs and the level of excitement rose one more notch. Who could it be? Who could possibly have memorised one hundred answers to one hundred random questions in order to win the prize? "And the winner is..." Mrs Baker made a fuss of opening the envelope and the crowd groaned, "...Simon ELLIS!"

Tumultuous applause ensued; children and teachers smiled and patted Simon on the back and he felt as though he would self-combust. The noise was unbearable, the clapping and cheering quite simply filled his brain until he thought he would faint. His head was spinning and when he went up to collect the trophy, it was sheer adrenaline which kept him from falling over. He, Simon Matthew Ellis, had won the GK100, the end of term general knowledge test. Each week, every student had to take home a sheet of paper with ten questions printed on it. They had to research the answers and then, on Thursday mornings, they would be tested, at random, on the answers. At the end of each term, everyone was tested on everything and on top of their usual homework, it was a really tall order.

"Right sweetie" said Simone, one evening, close to the end of term, "shall we have a go at your GK?"

"Do we have to?" asked a rather distracted Simon, who wanted to play with his Lego. His non-verbal abilities had been noted during the endless tests leading up to his autism diagnosis and at the age of just four, it was reckoned his Lego and brick building skills were that of the average eleven year old. When he started school, the older Year 2 boys would take the Lego and Stickle bricks outside and form a circle. Simon, who didn't really say much, even at the age of four, would sit in the middle and make things and they would watch with their mouths wide open. He was amazing. One day, his form teacher, Miss Tenby, watched from a safe distance, noted that, when he dismantled one thing, he would create something quite different, using exactly the same pieces and not one single piece would be left over. She could see he had special gifts, even if he didn't contribute much in class or speak to anyone.

"OK then, if I must," said Simon, stifling a yawn. His speech and language had come on in leaps and bounds in the past few years and although he had a special Learning Support Assistant with him during lessons, he really was coping so well, there was talk of him having support only during the more academic lessons and none during art, music or games. This was a massive step forward and Simone's heart sang as Simon's current teacher, Miss Briars, told her what wonderful strides her son had made throughout the year.

"Right, here we go sweetie. I won't ask the questions in order; that would be silly because they will test you by asking the questions in a totally different order. Capiche?"

"Capiche," said Simon. Oh well, if he had to do it, he might as well get on with it and then, he could go and watch one of his favourite dinosaur films.

"OK, here goes," said his rather worried mum. One hundred questions in no particular order would frazzle the cleverest person and she wondered whether he could cope.

"Which famous artist painted pictures of water lilies?"

"Don't know" said Simon.

"OK. I'll give you a clue. It begins with an 'M'"

"Oh I know, I know, it's Methuselah" he shouted, excitedly.

"Erm, no, not quite but I can see where you're coming from on that one sweetie."

Simon was muddling up the questions and the answers. He had memorised each answer but couldn't necessarily apply the correct one to the correct question. Had she asked them in the correct order, he would probably have rattled through them. In fact, some weeks, he would answer the question before she had asked it because he had memorised the entire sheet. His verbal skills might have been a long time coming but heck, he had a fantastic memory.

"Let's try another one" she said, crossing her fingers. She didn't want him to feel as though he wasn't doing well. Stupid GK, didn't the poor kids have enough to learn without this on top of everything else?

"Who was Miep Gies? Goodness, what an unusual name. Do you know this one, sweetie?"

"Yes, yes, I do, I know this one," said Simon, grinning because he was convinced he knew the answer, "wasn't she the brave lady who hid Anne Frank and her family from the Nazis during the American Civil War?"

Simone despaired. How on earth was he going to get through a hundred questions when he kept on muddling up the answers? "Why don't you go and watch your film, sweetie? I'll wash up and maybe we'll have another go at it later, before bed. They do say learning stuff at bedtime helps you to remember it in the morning."

Off he went, pleased to have been let off the hook. She left the questions in his room and suggested he have a good look at them before bedtime. Things, on the whole, were so much better. Simon was now able to dress himself and clean his own teeth although he hadn't quite mastered shoelaces and the poor games teacher found it all very difficult on a Wednesday afternoon. Most of the children were on the pitch while poor Simon was left struggling with his laces in the changing room. Still, small steps. Who would have thought he would even be able to read and remember the answers to all those questions every week. She just had to get him through the final test and then they could relax and enjoy the school holidays.

A week later, Simone was in the kitchen, trying to decide whether to have another soya milk coffee or an Earl Grey tea. She was daydreaming, trying to imagine the time Simon might be able to pack his own school bag or maybe even make himself a sandwich. She'd been so scared he would never be able to look after himself. He used to run out in front of cars and once, even vanished when they were in London. Her heart had stopped and she imagined herself on the news, begging for her son to be returned to her. Then, a security guard had frog-marched Simon over to her, asking in a very cross voice "Is he yours?" Oh! The relief, the sheer relief to have him back. She fell to her knees and wrapped her arms around him, saying "You're back, oh thank goodness you're back." He just stared over her shoulder, not knowing what all the fuss was about. Why was his mother crying and why was the man so cross? Simone took him for an ice cream and bought herself a very strong cappuccino. She would never take her eyes off him again. Ever.

(Dring, dring)

"Hello, is that Mrs Ellis? Simon's mother?"

"Erm, yes, yes it is, how can I help you?"

"It's Mrs Baker, Simon's Head Teacher."

"Oh yes, of course it is, I'm sorry, I was in a daydream. I thought I recognised your voice. Is everything OK? He's not in trouble is he?"

"No, no, nothing like that. I just thought you'd like to know that Simon has won the end of term General Knowledge competition. He got all one hundred answers right, even though the questions were set at random."

Simone sat down rather suddenly. She felt quite faint. Could she be hearing this correctly?

"Hello, hello...Mrs Ellis, are you still there?"

"Yes, yes I am. Thank you. Thank you so much. I don't know what to say. I'm quite overwhelmed, I had thought he..."

"Yes", interrupted Mrs Baker, "it's quite marvellous and indeed, a veritable testament to your hard work and dedication. We, in school, can tell how hard you work with Simon and he has come on in leaps and bounds this year. In fact, don't tell him yet, but we are all voting for The Best Improver next week and I have a sneaking feeling he might be a very strong contender. Well, goodbye for now Mrs Ellis and well done, you must be very proud."

Simone put the kettle on and made herself that cup of Earl Grey tea, nice and weak so you could see the bottom of the mug. She sat, staring out towards the garden and allowed herself a brief moment of pride. She knew it would be an uphill struggle to get Simon where he needed to be but this was absolutely amazing. He had actually won something. A test everyone wanted to win. The kudos of coming top in the GK100 was quite something and she was very much looking forward to greeting her surprising son at the school gates at four 'o clock.

She finished her tea, washed up the cup and walked to the hallway to put on her outdoor shoes. Nobody wore shoes on their carpets, it was one of her little foibles and if Simon had forgotten anything from his room, he would walk on his knees rather than be bothered with untying his shoelaces. His mum still did them up for him, it was their little secret. Simone gathered up her handbag and started to think about Simon's birthday, which was looming. She knew exactly what he would ask for and somehow, she had to persuade him that a trip to the Natural History Museum to see the animated dinosaurs was as good as owning his very own dog. He wouldn't agree of course but she was allergic and that was that. They couldn't have a dog so he was going to have to live with it.

Chapter Fifteen

(Dring dring...Dring dring...)

"Hello, Dogs Trust, how can I help you?" trilled Jemma.

"Oh hi," said Gareth, trying to word his question carefully. This was the fifth dog shelter he had called and he was beginning to feel rather like a parrot, asking the same question over and over again, "I don't suppose you have any black greyhounds there, do you?"

"Well, if you don't mind my asking," said Jemma, rather suspiciously, "that's a rather specific request. Are you thinking of adopting one?"

"No, well, yes, well, actually no but I am looking for one in particular." He didn't know how to explain the situation without getting himself and all his former friends into trouble. Would they demand lots of money to cover his food and shelter after all this time? If so, he wouldn't be able to afford it on his own and he presumed the others had long stopped thinking about the beautiful, black, shiny dog they'd once co-owned.

Jemma was a little worried and motioned to her deputy manager to listen in on the extension phone. Nobody rang up and asked for such a specific dog and if they did, the alarm bells immediately rang in her head. What if they wanted to race them or take them hare coursing? Greyhounds could still run very quickly, even when they were past their racing best. Of course, all ex-racers ready for adoption were spayed or neutered, to make sure nobody could breed from them but she had to be very careful when re-homing the 'greys'.

"Right, let's get this straight," said Jemma, pretending to write in the air to show her deputy that she wanted him to note anything this man said, "you are looking for a black greyhound. Does the dog have to be male or female or don't you mind which?"

"It has to be a male; around 32 kilogrammes, although of course, he may have lost weight since I last....erm... oh, and he should have four white socks and a white blaze down his chest."

"I don't suppose you'd know his ear tattoo numbers by any chance, would you?" She was being facetious but to her surprise, the man said "Well, erm, I used to know them. At least, I would have had them written down somewhere at some point...I suppose..." His voice tailed off and Jemma nodded knowingly at her deputy, Christian. "So, this is a dog you once knew then? Did he, by any chance, belong to you?"

He'd been rumbled and he slammed the phone down. Jemma looked across at Christian, who was still holding the extension phone with his mouth wide open. The man had just given a perfect description of the river dog. The one who'd come to their centre to be rehomed a few months ago. They'd found the owner and he'd just hung up on them. Jemma picked up the phone again and began dialling a number. Christian realised she was ringing the police to report the man but said "Don't you think we should give him a chance to explain? Maybe something absolutely terrible happened, maybe he was taken ill and couldn't look after the dog, who knows? We should, at least, allow him to explain. Dial 1471 to see what his number was."

Jemma dialled the number but shook her head. "Number withheld," she said, looking glum. Oh well, if the dog was important enough to him, maybe, just maybe, he might ring back and then, they could gently question him about his knowledge of this beautiful greyhound and find out exactly what happened to him before he'd fallen into the river.

Gareth was shaking. What had he done? They'd ring the police for sure if they thought he'd abandoned poor Hero. He could kick himself. Why hadn't he just left it all alone, carried on with his life and forgotten about the dog? He'd learned to live without Donna, surely he could carry on without some daft, injured dog weighing down on his conscience. He made a promise to himself NOT to ring them again. He'd withheld his number so they couldn't trace him. At least, he hoped they couldn't trace him. He would keep an eye out on the road, if any police cars passed by, he would make sure it looked as though he was out. Idiot. Total plonker. He might have caused himself no end of trouble had they known who he was.

Jemma rang Jenny, their nearest RGT representative and relayed the phone conversation. "Yup, I'm sure he was something to do with this dog. He knew too much about him and gave an almost perfect description of his markings, y'know, his white socks and blaze down his chest. He withheld his number so we can't trace him but if he rings back, I'll be sure to let you know."

Gareth poured himself a beer. He'd tried to find Hero and in trying, he'd possibly caused himself a lot of problems. He sipped the beer, turned on the telly and decided he would shut Handsome Hero out of his mind, forever.

Chapter Sixteen

"But what if I can't stop sneezing?" asked Simone

"Aw, come on Mum. You're always telling me to 'feel the fear but do it anyway'. What happened to my big brave mother?"

"Oi! Less of the 'big' and yes, of course, I will just have to be brave."

It wasn't exactly like owning a dog but, having won the GK100 quiz, Simon had managed to persuade his mother that a visit to the local dog shelter would be almost as good. He knew his mum was allergic to dogs, cats, horses, rabbits and every other fluffy creature known to mankind but he also knew you could take some kind of tablet which would help with the sneezing. Simone had been to the pharmacy and bought a packet of antihistamine tablets. She'd also bought one of those funny surgical masks which made her look really stupid but if it meant he was going to get to spend some time with real live dogs, Simon certainly wasn't going to tell her that.

It was Simon's birthday on the first day of the school holidays. His dad had sent him a cheap card with a picture of a boy kicking a football. The card didn't have any particular number on it, he wondered whether his father actually knew how old he was. He had seen Neil just once since he'd left, when he had come back to collect his remaining clothes and belongings. They'd sat on the bottom step of the stairs, Simon not being able to communicate much and Neil simply not knowing what to say to his silent, serious son. He'd patted him on the head before leaving for good and that night, Simon could hear his mum crying in her room. He didn't go in. He wouldn't have known what to do or what to say so it was best he just stayed in his own room, surrounded by his dinosaurs and trains.

"Right, birthday boy," said Simone "let's do this dogs' home thing." She turned the key in the ignition of their clapped out old banger, muttering the usual prayer 'Please start, please start' and was rewarded with a low, rather uncertain 'Brrrrrrrrr' as Lazarus grumbled to life. "Why do you call the car 'Lazarus' Mum?" Simon asked one day, "Because he keeps dying and then coming back to life" smiled Simone "Google him and you'll see what I mean." She began reversing out of their tiny driveway. "Mum, I don't think you need to wear the mask on the way to the Dogs Trust, only when you get there. Isn't it obscuring your vision?" "Ooh, get you with your big words," said Simone, her voice rather muffled through the mask, "and no, it is not obscuring my vision as you so eloquently put it, I am fine." They both groaned as a scraping noise came from the rear of the car; once again, Simone had managed to scrape the paintwork against the low wall. There really wasn't much room but she preferred to keep the old banger on the driveway, in case the local hoodlums tried to pull off the wing mirrors or scratched their cola can rings along the paintwork. She decided to take Simon's advice, removed her mask and they set off for the Dogs Trust.

Simon could barely contain his excitement and was wriggling like a worm in the front passenger seat. "Sweetie, you're making me feel seasick, could you keep still?" asked Simone, who really was very worried about having some sort of asthma attack at the dogs' home. "Sorry mother," said Simon, "It's just that I'm so excited. Really excited about seeing lots of dogs today. I wonder whether…" "Let me stop you right there," said his mum, "it ain't gonna happen so please don't get your hopes up. We cannot have a dog. Full stop."

Simon went quiet and made a promise to himself. If his mother (by any miracle) met a dog which didn't make her sneeze or wheeze and she (by another very large miracle) let him bring it home, he would do something very special for someone else. He would find a way of making someone else's life nicer or something like that. He didn't quite know how he would do this, he didn't really have any friends but if his mum made his life perfect by allowing him to have a non-allergenic dog, he would find a way.

"Look! Look!" he shouted "We're here! We're actually here. Where are the dogs? Where are the dogs?"

Simone had never seen her son so animated. If this was the effect dogs had on him, it was a real shame she had asthma; a dog might just be the ideal companion for her special, quirky son. "Well, I can't imagine they let them run loose, sweetie; there will be all sorts of breeds of dog and they might not all get along together. Let's go to the office and see what's what." She put on her mask and, after locking Lazarus with her key, they set off across the car park to a big five bar gate. The sign nailed to the gate said 'Welcome to Dogs Trust' and another said 'Office this way' with an arrow, pointing to a stable door at the end of a cobbled yard. They carefully closed the gate "We don't want the dogs to get out, do we?" asked Simone, her voice slightly wobbly now that they were almost in the presence of real, live, furry, four-legged animals.

"Hello," said the cheerful girl with the blonde hair, pretending not to notice the lady was wearing a surgical mask "How can I help you? My name's Jemma and I'm the manager of this Dogs Trust centre, are you looking to adopt a dog?"

"Yes please," said Simon.

"Erm, not really" said Simone, her voice sounding very odd through the mask, "I'm allergic you see, so I can't have a dog but as my lovely son here has won a competition in school and it's his birthday, as a treat, I've brought him along to just look at the dogs. I hope that's OK and we won't upset any of your inmates". Jemma smiled; it was funny how many people referred to the dogs as 'inmates', as though they were in a prison of some sort. The main aim was to get as many dogs homed as possible, not to keep them behind bars.

"Of course," she said, "That will be absolutely fine. We would ask that you go around the centre with Christian here, he's my deputy and he will show you around the place properly and introduce you to some of our (ahem) 'inmates'." Simon was practically doing a jig, hopping from foot to foot at the prospect of actually getting to stroke a dog. Christian smiled and said "Right, this way then, young man and oh, by the way…Happy Birthday to You, Happy Birthday to You, Happy Birthday dear… erm, what's your name?" "It's Simon," said Simon happily. "Dear Simon" continued Christian, in a very out of tune singing voice, "Happy Birthday TOOOO YO-OOOUUUU". Simon felt very special, rather like a VIP and the best thing was, in just a few seconds, he would come face to face with a real dog. He couldn't wait.

Simone couldn't decide whether or not to stay in the office but as there were two sleepy Labradors, snoozing on a squishy tartan bed in the corner, she would be subjected to doggy smells in any case so she decided to 'feel the fear and do it anyway' by following Christian and Simon through the metal gates and into the area where the dogs lived, mostly two to a pen but with the occasional solo occupant along the way. She had plenty of tissues at the ready, in case of a sneezing fit but as she had no intention of touching any of the dogs, she just kept them in her handbag.

"Oh Mum…LOOK!" shouted Simon in his 'I'm very excited' high pitched voice. "Shush sweetie, you don't want to frighten the dogs." whispered Simone, who was feeling quite light headed. She'd never been this close to so many dogs in her whole life. The noise was quite incredible; every single dog was barking and some were jumping up and down on their hind legs, noses pressed up against the wire mesh of their pens. Christian smiled across at Simone and said "I don't think you need worry about noise, this lot make more of a racket than any amount of children. Now then Simon, would you like to meet some dogs?" "Ooh, yes please" said Simon, his eyes wide, he was in doggy heaven; never, in his wildest dreams, could he have imagined how amazing his trip to the Dogs Trust would be.

"These two are called Samson and Delilah," said Christian, standing in front of a cage housing two tiny Chihuahuas, "They were brought in together because their owner had sadly, passed away." Simon frowned. Sometimes people talked in riddles and he didn't understand what they meant. Why couldn't everyone just speak normally? He looked up quizzically at his mum. She, realising he didn't understand the phrase 'passed away', whispered quietly "The person who owned the dogs has died." Simon wondered why Christian hadn't just told him that; the world was a funny place and people were very strange at times. "Oh, that's very sad," said Simon, "I hope someone will adopt them both, it would be awful if they had to go to two different homes." "Oh, you needn't worry about that," said Christian, "they will be re-homed together, it would be cruel to separate them after all the years they've spent together. Anyway, let's face it, they don't take up much room do they?" Simon looked hopefully up at his mother; she pretended not to notice.

The continued walking around the pens. There were Labradors, liver and white spaniels, German Shepherds and even a lovely Saluki with a fluffy tail. Then, Simon spotted a big black dog in a pen all on his own. He wasn't jumping up and down like the other dogs, he was lying on his bed, his big brown eyes staring blankly through the mesh of the cage. "Why isn't that one jumping around?" asked Simon. "Ah, that's River," said Christian, "he's been here quite a while and nobody really shows much interest in him because he's quite a bit bigger than the average family pet. I think he's a bit depressed because nobody really wants to adopt him. We think he was injured some time ago and his back legs are a bit wobbly so visitors tend to pass by his pen on the way to the smaller dogs."

"He's beautiful," said Simon, staring at River "so beautiful, isn't he Mum?" Simone pretended to be examining the wire mesh at the front of a cage, she was a bit frightened of dogs and this one was enormous. "Why do you call him 'River'?" Simon asked Christian, "That's a funny name for a dog." "It's a long story," said Christian "he was found in the river, you know, the one on the other side of the dual carriageway." Simon wasn't sure what a dual carriageway was, he just wanted to know all about this beautiful, black, sad looking dog so he just nodded and carried on staring at River. "We think he must be an ex-racing dog" continued Christian, "he has ear tattoos but one ear is rather torn so we can't make out the numbers. He also has dodgy back legs which means he was probably injured during a race. Either way, he's had a hard time of it; it would be lovely if we could find him his 'furever' home, do you see what I did there?" He nudged Simon to see whether he'd understood the joke but Simon hadn't heard, he was totally mesmerised and couldn't take his eyes off River.

He had such beautiful eyes and a really sad face. Simon wasn't very good at empathising with others, one of the reasons he found making friends so difficult but his heart went out to the huge black dog, it must be very lonely in his pen, all by himself. The staff had thrown in a few cuddly toys but they lay unused in the corner of the concrete pen. Greyhounds are not used to playing or fun. They eat, they drink, they train and they race. They are not like other dogs who are bred as pets; they are bred to win races so fun isn't something they understand. It would take a very special family to understand how to socialise a dog who'd never really been petted or made a fuss of.

Simone coughed and said "Shouldn't we be going Simon, sweetie? You have lots of holiday homework to do and it's getting a bit late." Simon didn't even hear his mum's voice. He walked across to River's pen and said "Hello boy, Hello River." The dog didn't move but his ears pricked up slightly. He didn't really know the name he'd been given by the Dogs Trust staff so it didn't have any effect on him but he did recognise a kind voice. "River, River, c'mon boy." said Simon, softly. Simone panicked and said "Simon! We really do have to go NOW." "Mum, purleez, it's my birthday treat, we've only just arrived. Couldn't I just talk to him for a minute, he's so sad and I think he needs cheering up?"

Christian smiled and asked Simone "Are you nervous?" She looked embarrassed and realised she must appear stupid, wearing a surgical mask and fiddling with her handbag to try and calm her nerves. She removed the mask and took a deep breath; if her son wasn't scared, she needed to get a grip and the dogs were all locked in their pens, they couldn't hurt her. Simon was in a world of his own and had persuaded River to get up off his bed and come to the wire mesh. The dog had positioned his head so Simon could scratch behind his ear and although he was a long way off from actually wagging his tail, something told him this boy was friendly and he stood very still, enjoying the feeling of Simon's fingers scratching his fur.

Simone motioned to Christian and they both walked further down the line of pens. The dogs had mostly calmed down and she could hear herself speak this time. "Simon has autism and although I would love for him to have his very own dog, I am allergic to just about everything with fur so it's just not going to be possible I'm afraid. Today was a birthday treat, just a trip to look at the dogs. We couldn't possibly consider taking one home with us." Christian listened carefully and then said "I have a friend with the most dreadful allergies. She's allergic to most breeds of dog, cats, rabbits and she can't even talk to a horse over a fence without sneezing. She does, however, have three ex-racing greyhounds and so far, she's never suffered a sneezing fit or asthma. She adopted them all from us so I think I'd know if she had a problem."

Simone looked at her son, he was entranced by this sad, lonely dog. They both clearly needed a pal, someone they could spend time with, feel comfortable with. She was torn. If it was true and greyhounds wouldn't make her sneeze, then she should at least consider adopting one for Simon. She decided she would think about it long and hard without mentioning anything to him. "Come on sweetie, we really do have to go now." Simon reluctantly stopped stroking behind River's ear and walked away from the pen. River stood quite still, hoping Simon would come back. He watched the boy and his mother walk away, through the metal gates and padded slowly back to his bed, wincing as he lowered his back legs. Life was pretty boring in the pen but having someone stroke his ears had been nice. He watched for a while but, realising the boy had gone, he put his nose on his paws and settled down for another snooze.

Chapter Seventeen

Simon had not stopped talking about River for over a week, he talked about him even more than train timetables and dinosaurs and although Simone had had grave doubts about encouraging her son's interest in the big, black dog with the four white socks, she could see the effect he had on her son so she decided to take him for a second visit.

"Hello there," said Christian, "welcome back to Dogs Trust, it's really good to see you again. Oooh, now then, let me guess...you'd like to come and say 'Hello' to River again." Simon was hopping from foot to foot and he squeaked "Yes please" so Christian collected the key to the double metal gates and motioned to Simon to follow him. Simone held back, not quite sure what to do. The Labradors were not in the office today so she could easily just sit and wait there for her impossibly excited son. "Jemma's taken them for a walk" explained Christian, "they came to us when their owners emigrated to Australia and we all loved them so decided they would become our very own dogs. They're a good advert for Dogs Trust because they're lovely and gentle and everyone who visits loves them. Jemma takes them home every evening and they come into work with her whenever she's on duty, they're no trouble really." "Come on Mum," said Simon "don't you want to say 'Hello' to River again? Christian says he won't make you sneeze. Come on Mum, feel the fear…" "…and do it anyway" finished Simone. She realised she was being a bit pathetic and so, Aloe Vera tissues in hand, she followed Simon and Christian through the gates and into the area where the noise of the barking would have drowned out the most allergic person's sneezing fit.

"Hello boy; hello River," said Simon, running across to the greyhound's pen. River, recognising the boy's voice, got up off his bed as quickly as his damaged legs would allow and hobbled across to the wire mesh. His big brown eyes looked up at Simon, he recognised the kind voice and remembered the lovely ear cuddles he'd had last time so he pushed his left ear as close as he could towards the mesh. Simon tickled him, as he had done on his first visit and he sighed a huge sigh; he really did like this dog and being with him made him feel as though he had 'come home' in a funny sort of way. He felt a connection with him that he'd never felt with anyone else, not even his mum.

Christian smiled at Simone and said "I think River's a hit with your boy. It's lovely to see them together, nobody has shown this much interest in him since he arrived. He's a lovely dog but we couldn't let him live in the office with us because he's an instinctive hunter, having been trained to chase from such a young age." Simone gave a watery smile, she was worried she'd done the wrong thing, allowing Simon to come back and visit the dog a second time. She was giving him the wrong signals and now, he would want to come back a third time. Who knows where it would end?

"Mum, could we take River for a walk? Please Mum, please?" Simon looked so expectant, so hopeful and this dog clearly made him very happy so she shrugged her shoulders and said "Christian, do you think we would cope with him? He's very big, I am guessing he's quite strong too." Christian grinned and said "Jemma will be back in a tick so I'll come with you if you like. Then I can show you how to put on his muzzle and collar." "His muzzle?" Simone's eyebrows vanished up underneath her fringe, she hadn't realised the flippin' thing had to be muzzled. "Yes," said Christian, "he's an ex-racing dog and although he has injuries, his brain will instantly go into 'chase mode' if he sees a small dog or a rabbit. It's just a safety precaution, he won't mind because he was always muzzled at the race track. I'll be back in a tick."

Christian walked back to the office to check Jemma was back behind the desk. He walked over to the hooks on the wall and chose a suitable muzzle, a special greyhound collar (wider than normal as their necks are quite slim) and a strong, leather lead. Meanwhile, Simon could barely breathe. He was going to take River on a walk. He was actually going to be allowed to hold the lead all by himself. Simone had her tissues at the ready, she could almost feel a sneeze coming on, even though the dog was still in his mesh fronted kennel. Christian came back and opened the door of River's pen. The dog wagged his tail, he liked his walks. The freedom was wonderful and even though he couldn't walk too far or too quickly, the feeling of being away from his pen and his bed was amazing. Christian slipped the muzzle over his long, pointy nose and carefully did up his collar, right behind his ears, to make sure he couldn't wriggle out backwards if he saw something he wanted to chase. Christian suggested walking River himself, just until they were on the other side of the yard. It was a quiet day, only a couple of volunteers had turned up to walk the dogs but he couldn't risk one of them appearing with a Yorkie or a Westie and River going into 'hunting mode'. Simon was impatient but realised this was going to be his only option. He and his mum walked alongside River and Christian; River was so tall, he came up to Simon's waist and he couldn't wait to get his hands on the lead so he could walk along with this beautiful dog and pretend he was actually his.

Simone walked as close to River as she dared. Nothing. Not a sneeze. Yet. She watched as Christian handed Simon the leather lead and felt her heart lurch as she saw his (often serious) face, burst into a huge smile. He was in heaven, no doubt about that. This was the one thing which would make her precious son's life complete, his very own dog and for some reason, he had bonded with an enormous, rather damaged ex-racing dog. Life was very strange at times.

"Do you want to hold him Mum?" asked Simon, "he's very good, he doesn't pull at all." "Erm, no, thanks, you're OK sweetie," she said tentatively, watching her son walk this huge dog was one thing but holding the lead herself was inconceivable "anyway, you're having a lovely time with him, make the most of it." Simon's face clouded over, what did she mean by that?

They strolled around the field behind the shelter, it was a lovely sunny day and because there were no other dogs in the field, Christian took River's muzzle off. "There, that's better, isn't it boy? I know he's used to being muzzled but I imagine it must feel lovely when it's taken off." River stopped walking and gave a huge shake and Simone hid behind Christian. He laughed and said "They do that all the time, it's a greyhound thing."

The walk was over all too soon and the three of them made their way back to the yard. Christian slipped River's muzzle back over his nose and took the leather lead from Simon as they approached the metal gates. "There, did you enjoy that Simon?" He could see that River and Simon were a match made in heaven but he could also see that Simon's mum was not at all comfortable around the dog. "Why don't you both come back on Saturday and we'll all take him out again?" Simon looked up at his mum, his eyes pleading with her. She sighed and said "OK then, I suppose so. If it makes you happy sweetie." "Thanks Mum," said Simon, giving her a huge hug "you're the best mum in the whole world." Hugs from her son were rare, he didn't like being touched or touching others and so Simone knew he must be very excited about his impending third visit to see River.

They set off home; Simon found it hard to tear himself away from his new four-legged friend and felt utterly miserable as he watched Christian put River back in his pen. "He'll be fine," said Christian, "it'll be tea time soon and once he's eaten, he'll settle down for a lovely nap." Simone and Simon drove in silence. "I know what you're thinking," said Simone "and it's very early days but so far, I haven't felt a sneeze coming on. I walked quite close to him so may next time, I'll try holding the lead and we'll see what effect he has on me." Simon didn't dare respond, it might just jinx the whole thing so he kept quiet until they got indoors and then, offered to make his mum a cup of tea. "Really?" she smiled, "you never make me cups of tea. What is it you want exactly, sweetie?" He grinned and filled the kettle; his mum knew exactly what he wanted but he had no idea whether she would go with it. He decided to play things cool and not to go on and on about River all evening. It would be difficult, it was all he thought about. Even more than dinosaurs and train timetables. If his mum would let him adopt River, he would never be unhappy ever again. He just knew it.

Simon didn't usually say prayers but that night, he prayed as he had never prayed before. "Please let Mum let me have River. Please, please, please. He's so beautiful and he's so lonely and I just know he and I could be the best of friends. Amen." Simone sat, watching a soap opera, not really taking in the plot. She wondered whether she might be going mad. From saying Simon couldn't have a dog, she was now contemplating letting him have the biggest dog she'd ever seen in her life. How on earth she would feed him, she had no first clue but she knew it would make Simon very happy and that was her main mission. That and paying the bills. Adopting a huge dog would push them up even further and she sighed to herself as she walked to the kitchen, made a cup of tea and wondered how life had become so complicated.

Chapter Eighteen

"'ere, Smellis" shouted Jecko who was leaning up against the wall outside the mini-mart on the High Street. Simon was walking River home from the park and hadn't seen his nemesis lurking outside the shop. He didn't want to risk the walk being ruined by Jecko's stupid comments so he began walking a little faster, hoping poor River could keep up with him. Now he was enjoying regular walks, his back legs seemed to have improved slightly. Lying on his bed for much of the day at the shelter meant his muscles weren't having to work and because most people had walked straight past his pen, in search of puppies or the more obviously family friendly dogs, he had long stopped bothering to get up and greet the visitors. It was such an effort to haul himself to his feet, he tended to stay on his bed because nobody had seemed that interested in him. Except Simon.

Simon had come back, time and time again, to visit his new black, silky headed pal. Simone had become quite friendly with Christian and Jemma and would have a cup of tea with them in the office while Simon excitedly put River's collar, lead and muzzle on him before taking him up to the field for a leisurely stroll. He would talk to River the whole time, which was unusual for Simon because in school, he rarely spoke to anyone unless he was answering a question in class. Since winning the GK100, Simon had gained some 'street-cred' and pupils who once ignored or teased him would sometimes stop for a chat. Trouble was, Simon wasn't good at talking about nothing in particular and so they would soon get bored, trying to prise some social chit-chat out of him.

"Hiya Mr Clever Clogs," said Ellie, one of the girls in his class "you must have a huge brain to have remembered all those answers in the GK100. Or did you cheat?"

"Cheat?" asked Simon, looking horrified, "No, I didn't cheat. Why would I cheat?"

Everything was black and white in Simon's world. Winning the GK quiz by cheating would never even occur to him; why would he cheat? What would be the point in winning the prize if he hadn't won it fair and square?

"Well" laughed Ellie, "some people think you must have hidden some answers up your sleeve or maybe done that thing where you write answers on your chewing gum, copy them out and then destroy the evidence by eating it."

"Eat chewing gum covered in lead?" asked Simon incredulously, did people really do such things? How disgusting.

Ellie was getting nowhere fast with this conversation so she decided to go and practice the violin. Ellie was good at everything. She invariably came top in the exams, played the violin, sang like an angel and could chat to anyone about anything. How marvellous that must be, mused Simon, to be able to just strike up a conversation with anyone you happened to pass in the playground. He had been known to stand, staring at the ground when someone had tried talking to him about the latest TV shows or Nintendo games. He hadn't a clue and the other person usually just gave up and wandered off. Still, his mum had finally caved in and allowed him to bring River home for a visit. It had gone quite well until River had walked into the glass doors which lead from the lounge to the tiny garden. Simon ran to the doors and sat on the floor, stroking River's head for a long time, talking to him, soothing him and trying to make sure he was OK. Simone watched in wonder. Simon had never been so attached to anyone before. He really appeared to love this dog, he cared about him more than he cared about himself. He was so 'in tune' with River, she couldn't see how she could possibly say 'No' if and when he asked about adopting him permanently. He hadn't asked yet but she knew he would.

"Does it bite?" asked Jecko, sneering across at Simon from the mini-mart wall. He was obviously bored and had nothing to do and nobody else to annoy. "Why's it got a cage over its face?"

"Erm, no...it, erm he doesn't bite. Greyhounds don't, as a rule, bite humans. They are natural hunters and instinctively chase small animals running away from them but on the whole, I think they quite like us. He's wearing a muzzle in case we see a small dog or a cat or a squirrel or something he might chase." Simon carried on walking but Jecko wanted a closer look at River. Surely something so big and impressive couldn't belong to that little squirt. He started following them; Simon walked a bit faster but he could feel River lagging behind and because he loved the dog more than he disliked Jecko, he slowed down and hoped the bully would soon get bored and go away.

"When you've finished givin' me a lecture 'bout greyhounds, can I touch it, erm him?" asked Jecko, who had caught up and was now walking right behind River and Simon.

Simon stopped and being a very well trained dog, so did River. "Well, if you promise not to hurt him or scare him, you can touch his head. You must be very gentle with him though" said Simon with some authority, "he's only just come from the Dogs Trust and hasn't been a pet for very long." Simon had finally won the battle and Simone had, with many misgivings, allowed him to bring River home for good on the proviso that he worked hard in school and walked the dog twice a day. Simon promised on his mother's life and then, realising what he'd said, changed his mind and said "If you let me have River, I will be the best and most brilliant son you could ever have hoped for." "You already are, my darling", smiled Simone and got out her phone to call Christian to tell him the good news.

"The Dogs Trust" questioned Jecko, "what's that when it's at 'ome then?" He wasn't that interested but he figured if he pretended to be fascinated by what Smellis had to say, he might get the chance to get closer to the dog. It really was a beautiful dog; black, silky and shiny and Jecko had never seen a greyhound close up before.

"Founded in 1891, Dogs Trust is the largest dog welfare charity in the UK. Their mission is to bring about the day when all dogs can enjoy a happy life, free from the threat of unnecessary destruction." Simon had learned all about the Dogs Trust online and, being Simon, had memorised each and every word.

"Yeah, yeah, yeah….yadda, yadda, yadda…" drawled Jecko, "is you goin' to let me 'old it or what?"

"I will let you hold him for a minute," said Simon, deciding that this was his moment to stand up to Jecko, "but you have to promise me that you will leave me alone in school. Your bullying has made me really unhappy, really miserable and that, in turn, has really upset my mum. Calling me names, laughing at me in the playground and allowing your horrible friends to do the same has made my life a total misery. If you will make me that promise, you can walk my dog, MY dog, for a few minutes. Is that OK?" His voice was wavering a bit. Jecko could be quite scary and he didn't want to make things in school any worse for himself.

"Yeah, whatevah" said Jecko, reaching for the lead, "I wuz gettin' a bit fed up wiv tormentoring you in any case, you ain't much fun to tease 'cuz you never bites back does ya?"

Simon's heart jumped; had he done it? Had he finally managed to get Jecko and his cronies off his back?

"You have to promise me you'll not only leave me alone but that you won't find anyone else to pick on or I'm taking River straight home now."

"Erm…" Jecko was confused, it was normally him telling Smellis what to do, "erm, well, awright I s'pose." His voice tailed off. He hadn't realised picking on Simon was making him so miserable, it was just a bit of fun, wasn't it?

Simon looked Jecko straight in the eye and handed him River's lead. "Take it slowly, he has been badly injured and can't walk very quickly. For once, you need to think about someone else and not yourself." Simon felt as though he was having some sort of 'out-of-body-experience'. Was he really laying down the law to Jecko the Bully Boy? Jecko seemed fascinated by River and wanted to walk him so much, he just agreed with everything Simon said. They all trotted along together in silence. Simon decided to try and start a conversation. If he had to learn to do it, he might as well start with someone who wouldn't be too much of a challenge.

"So, how are you today?"

"Eh?" Jecko looked at him, wondering whether he was having a funny turn "how am I? What's it to you, Smell…erm, Simon?"

"Well, I just wondered how you are. Isn't that how most people start a conversation, asking one another how the other one is? I've always thought that was a bit stupid but my mum says it's a good way to start chatting with someone."

"Your mum knows everyfink don't she?" sneered Jecko "maybe I should ask her for the next lot of winnin' lottery numbers." He cackled at his own stupid joke and Simon went quiet. Jecko, despite his bluff manner, realised he had pushed Simon too far. "Erm, what I meant was that your mum seems interested in you and the fings you do. Mine ain't bovvered about me at all. I don't even know where she is. She could be darn the pub or at the bingo. No first clue. I 'spect she'll come home when she runs out of dosh."

Simon was shocked. Did Jecko really not know where his mum was? That was inconceivable to Simon. His mum was either at home, making his breakfast, burning his dinner or running him a bath. Or she was at her part-time job, trying to make enough money to pay the bills and now, of course, to pay for the dog food. Thankfully, River didn't eat much, he tended to graze rather like a cat and there was often food left in his bowl during the day.

"What do you mean, you don't know where your mum is? Surely she's at home, isn't she?" Jecko laughed but Simon, although he didn't read social signals well, could tell it wasn't a happy laugh. "Young Smellis me laddo, oops, I mean Simon me laddo, you must be kidding! My muvver ain't given two monkeys about me since me dad left 'er when I wuz a kid. She ain't never at 'ome, I 'ardly sees 'er from one day to the next. I 'ad to buy some crisps from the shop for me dinner, I'm starving hungry and there ain't nuffink in the fridge at 'ome."

Simon actually felt sorry for Jecko. Jecko the Bully, the older boy who had made his life an absolute misery ever since he started secondary school. At least he, Simon, had a lovely mum who really cared about him and helped him with his homework. A mum who tried her best to cook nice meals for him (mostly failing, but at least she tried) and made him laugh every day. She had also let him adopt River, something he had never thought would happen. She must really love him and here was poor Jecko with a mum who was rarely at home and didn't care two hoots about where he was or wht he was doing.

"My dad left home too," said Simon, as they turned into the road where he lived.

"Did he?" asked Jecko, "why's that then?"

"Well, my mum told me I've got something called autism and that my dad couldn't understand it and blamed himself or something, so off he went. I haven't seen him for years."

"Nah, me neither," said Jecko, "my old man scarpered when I was just two years old, I don't even remember what he looks like. What's autism then? Is it an illness?"

"No, I don't think so," said Simon, wondering how to explain it to Jecko, "it's a sort of thing where I don't always get jokes. I can't always tell what people are thinking just from looking at their faces. I find bright lights very annoying and my mum has to cut all the labels out of my jumpers and shirts because they drive me mad and I can't concentrate on anything if they are scratching my skin. I don't know how to talk to people about nothing, I need something definite to talk about like dinosaurs or train timetables or Dogs Trust stuff, I find all that kind of thing very interesting but I can't just talk unless I have a subject to talk about."

It was as though a light bulb had switched on above Jecko's head. That's why Smellis...erm, Simon... couldn't eat food if it had been placed on the wrong side of the plate or if different foods had been mixed together. He wasn't weird, it was something called autism. He had heard of it but he didn't know what it was or how it worked. Simon had just explained how the world appeared to someone with autism and Jecko felt suddenly ashamed. He had teased Simon mercilessly about his lunch that day and Jecko cringed to remember just how far he had pushed him. He went quiet and they carried on walking towards Simon's house.

"Right, we're here now," said Simon, "Can I have River's lead back please?" Jecko hadn't realised he'd walked River the whole way back to Simon's house and he reluctantly handed back the leather leash. "Erm, could I...erm, can I...could we take him out for a walk again tomorrow?" Simon almost gasped, was this Jecko or had someone kidnapped him and replaced him with a normal, fairly nice person? "Well, I do need to take him on two short walks a day so I suppose I will be out at some point tomorrow so if you're around, that's fine." Jecko made a mental note to make himself available for a walk the following day. "Right, see ya then Smelli... erm, Simon. Bye River, bye, thanks for the walk."

Simon stood and watched as Jecko walked away. He cut a lonely figure in his ill-fitting second-hand clothes, wandering back to an empty house with nobody waiting for him, no-one to make him a milky drink at bedtime or to put his pyjamas on the radiator to warm them before he hopped into bed. Maybe Jecko, like River, needed a friend, mused Simon. Who'd have thought adopting a dog would improve matters between him and the school bully?

Simone was waiting at the lounge window. She smiled as she saw Simon and River walk up the pathway. "Hello sweetie," she said as she opened the front door, "how was your walk?" "Very nice" said Simon "but the strangest thing happened. You will never guess, in a million years, who ended up walking with us?" Simone's heart skipped a beat, "Not your dad?" she asked quickly, she hadn't seen him for ages and didn't really want to re-ignite that old flame. "No, don't be daft," said Simon, taking off River's muzzle and lead, "it was Jecko. You know, that boy who used to make fun of me in school and call me names. He wanted to get close to River so I let him walk him back home. It was really weird. He was almost nice to me." "Ooer" said Simone, glad it wasn't her ex-husband who'd accompanied Simon on the walk. Not that she didn't want Simon to see him, she just wasn't ready to confront that particular ghost just yet.

"Right sweetie. What's for dinner do you think? A) Snails on toast B) Worm burgers or C) Stir fry?" "Muuuuuuum, not another multiple choice question. Purleez!" Simon went to wash his hands in readiness for dinner but not before checking his precious pet had a full bowl of fresh water. River took a lovely long drink and then wandered over to his duvet, rearranged it as only greyhounds do, creating a big squashy mountain and plonking himself down in the middle of it for a snooze. Simon was feeling very happy this evening. His lovely mum had attempted one of his favourite dinners and managed not to ruin it, his beautiful dog was asleep on his bed and the boy who'd made his life so miserable for so long had finally backed off. Could his life get any better?

Chapter Nineteen

Gareth poured himself another glass of cheap red wine. It was Friday evening and he had just finished a week's freelance work. He was a very capable IT engineer and the money he'd earned would help pay the bills for another month. He hated living hand-to-mouth but since leaving his permanent job, after the racetrack disaster, he'd found it difficult to concentrate and any interviews he'd had, had not gone well because he was so depressed about Hero's accident and had no idea what had happened to the dog. There had been no repercussions after his call to the Dogs Trust; nobody had come looking for him so he decided to leave well enough alone and concentrate on getting a job and possibly getting his love life back on track. He registered with an agency who sent out IT qualified engineers on an ad hoc basis, a few days or weeks at a time. He also registered with a well-known online dating agency, posted a reasonable photo of himself smiling at the camera with a glass of champagne in his hand and crossed his fingers someone would send him a 'nudge' and want to chat.

His phone pinged. Someone wanted to chat, that was quick! He sat down with his glass of wine and opened up the e-mail. A girl smiled out from his phone screen; dark hair, nice eyes, slim. This was looking good so he had a look at her profile. Her name was Angie, she was thirty four and she worked as a manager at a well-known supermarket. He clicked 'Yes' and sent a one-liner, pre-written for him by the dating agency. 'I think we could be a perfect couple, let's talk' and waited for her response.

Two days later, he found himself standing outside 'The Greyhound' pub (oh, the irony), feeling quite nervous about his first date with Angie. What if he couldn't think of anything to talk about? It had all been so easy with Donna; he could bang on about Hero, his racing stats, how much he'd won in prize money recently and to be honest, Donna did most of the talking in any case. She'd been a 'user' but he still missed her and her high pitched Rhondda accent, her obsession with EastEnders and the way she pulled his leg when he tried to comb his hair over his bald patch.

Then, he spotted her. Angie. Oh no! She was at least ten years older than her photo and what's more, she was not the slim, dark haired girl he'd hoped to meet in person. Well, her hair was very dark but unfortunately, her roots were not and they gave her away immediately. She was at least five stone heavier in real life and he froze. What to do? Run? Hide? She'd obviously seen him because she had broken into a disconcerting trot and in between making 'puff, puff' noises, she was trying to shout "Cooeeeee". People were staring at her and he just wanted the ground to swallow him up. "Puff, puff, puff...hello...puff, puff, puff...I'm Angie...

puff, puff...you must be...puff, puff...Gareth...puff, puff..." "Erm, hi" he stammered "yes, that's right, that's me, the very same. Erm, shall we?" and he pointed to the pub door, hoping she would take an instant dislike to him and want to go home early.

The date lasted an uncomfortable hour and a half, most of which Gareth spent staring into his pint glass and wishing he were at home, watching telly. Instead, he had to listen to Angie bang on about her auntie's budgie's broken beak, her incredibly boring job and how she would retire to Tenerife if she won the lottery. "I don't buy a ticket or nuffink" (Angie screeched with laughter at her own jokes) "but I've always liked the idea of living in the sunshine and lounging around the pool all day." Gareth was tired and he was fed up and just as he felt Angie was settling in for the whole evening, he did something quite out of character. He asked her why she had posted such an old photo of herself. "Well, 'scuse me," she said, her eyes glittering dangerously, "is that the only fing wot's important to you? Looks?" He baulked and started back peddling, he didn't really want to fight with her, he just wanted her to leave so he could go home and he could have bitten his tongue for being so stupid. "Erm, well, you look nice now of course but you look quite erm, different from the way you looked back then. I just wondered why you didn't post a current photo?" Angie threw her drink over him, burst into tears and stormed out of the pub. Unfortunately, her rather generous build meant she got stuck in the swinging doors and had to be released by a passing barman before she could escape.

Gareth sucked his teeth; what was he doing here? Why didn't life just throw him a straight ball from time to time? Other pub customers were staring at him, he was covered in yellow gloop (Angie had ordered a double Advocaat and Lime) and he couldn't have looked more pathetic if he'd tried. It was only half past seven but he drank the remainder of his pint, stood up, gave a lop-sided smile at the barman and walked towards the door. "Floor show's over folks" he shouted as he left the pub and got out his car keys. He might have to sell the car if things didn't look up soon but for now, he hoped he would get home on the thimbleful of petrol he'd put in earlier that day. He decided to take the shortest route; he usually drove past the garage to buy some cans of beer but he was pretty sure the petrol wouldn't get him home if he took the detour this evening. It was June and still light outside. Somehow, getting home when it was still light felt wrong. He should be out, partying like he used to in the good old days. He sighed, turned the key in the ignition and set off back to his lonely, rented flat.

He stopped at the red traffic light, pulled up the rather unreliable handbrake and fiddled with the car radio, trying to find some uplifting music to cheer himself up. He heard the 'Beep beep beep' as the pedestrian light turned green and glanced up to see whether anyone was crossing. There were two boys, both in their teens and walking slowly in between them was a big, black grey-hound. A big black greyhound with four white socks. Gareth's heart skipped a beat. The dog was walking as though its back legs weren't working properly. The traffic light turned green and the driver behind beeped his car horn very loudly. "OK, OK," said Gareth, "keep your wig on" and he slowly turned the car to the right instead of going straight on towards his flat, hoping it didn't look as though he was following the boys and their dog. He prayed they would arrive home soon, (he knew the fiver's worth of fuel wouldn't go very far) and then, he could clock the house number and maybe call by to see if it really was Hero. He couldn't think of any good reason to call on a family he didn't know but he would think of something.

The boys stopped walking and started chatting to one another so Gareth pulled his car over, pretending to be looking for directions on his phone. He wound his window down and heard the older boy say "Right, see ya' tomorrow then" and the younger one respond "OK, see you tomorrow" before opening the garden gate to number seven. The property had a very small driveway which housed a battered old maroon coloured car. It was badly scratched at the back, he guessed the driver had scraped it on the low wall a few times. A woman waved at the boy from the lounge window and then, opened the front door to him. The other boy had walked off so clearly, he didn't live there. He wondered whether there was a man living at the property, he didn't want to have to deal with a big, burly husband but he had to know whether the dog was Hero.

"Think, think, think Gareth. What to do now?" he muttered to himself. The dog's height, unmistakable white socks and blaze down his chest told him it had to be Hero and his back legs didn't look right at all. He would go home and have a think about how to approach the people who lived at number seven. He drove home, poured himself a small glass of wine, sat on his uncomfortable sofa and planned what to do next. If it was Hero, he would so love to see him again, to stroke his silky head and to say how sorry he was for abandoning him in his hour of need. He just needed to find a reason to go tapping on the front door of number seven.

Chapter Twenty

"So, that's that then," said Jemma, snapping shut her laptop lid, "we've finally found a home for River. It's been a long haul, hasn't it? I was beginning to think we'd never find the right person to take him on. I do hope he'll be OK. I know Simon loves him, I just hope his mum will help look after River if and when he finds it all a bit of a chore. Kids these days don't seem to have the staying power we had."

"Hark at grandma" laughed Christian, flipping the kettle switch to 'On', "I doubt she will need to do that much. Based on what I know about Simon, he's a good kid and he will do his best to look after River. Don't they say autistic people are really focused and enjoy routine? If that's the case, River should be the best cared for dog in the world."

"Autistic? Is Simon autistic? How on earth do you know that?" asked Jemma. Christian never failed to amaze her with his inside knowledge of their adopters.

"Well, all it takes is a good pair of ears and over the weeks he came to visit, he did or said certain things which made me wonder."

"Like what?" she asked as she opened up the bottom filing cabinet drawer to put away River's adoption papers "name me one thing you spotted which shouted 'autistic' at you."

"Well, he would always check the bolt was drawn across the metal gates whenever we went in to see the dogs. He never once just walked through and didn't check it and he would slide it open and shut at least twice to make sure it was definitely secure. He didn't know what 'passed away' meant when I told him about Samson and Delilah, his mum had to explain that it meant 'dead'. I think that was the real giveaway, I realised I needed to be quite black and white with him, no pussyfooting around with metaphors or similes so talking to him got quite a bit easier once I realised that. Also, I don't know whether you noticed but he didn't always look straight at the person he was talking to. He would often stare over my shoulder, almost as though he couldn't listen to me and look at me at the same time. I had a hunch about him and so I started reading about autism online after I'd met him a couple of times. Interestingly, it said they sometimes find it difficult to make eye contact whilst listening to someone speak. It was as though he needed to look away in order to 'see' my voice. Sounds very odd I know, but that's how it felt."

"Well, whatever you did, it worked and I was really chuffed when his mum said they would take him permanently" smiled Jemma, trying to decide whether or not to pop into the village shop for some sandwiches. "You really are very good with visitors; that's why I let you do the talking and then, I take all the credit when we organise the actual adoption." Christian winked at Jemma, he liked her, she worked hard and she really cared about the dogs. "If you're popping into the village, could you buy me some sarnies?" he asked, "anything veggie would be good." "Ewww" Jemma winced, "I don't know how you do it, I couldn't eat veggie food the whole time, it just isn't natural." "Well, it works for me" he said, "I can't imagine eating meat ever again and don't go giving me that thing about 'I-bet-you-miss-bacon-sandwiches' because I don't. I know what they are made from and I simply couldn't eat one now." "OK, OK" she laughed, "I promised not to mention bacon sarnies if you'll do me a favour and call the vet's surgery while I'm out. Just let them know we've homed River and tell them we've given Simone Ellis their number in case his back legs don't improve as well as we'd hoped. I'm guessing that, with gentle daily walks, he will do very well but they need to keep an eye on him and I was very impressed with the way they put poor old River back together again."

She gathered up her handbag, sunglasses and car keys and set off towards the car park. Christian sat back in his swivel chair with his hands behind his head and stretched his legs out underneath the desk. He really liked his job and he was absolutely thrilled River was no longer living alone in his pen, sadly watching the visitors walk past the wire mesh and rarely stopping to talk to him. Simon was a quirky boy and somehow, Christian had always known he and River were meant for each another. Things really couldn't have turned out any better, for either of them. The phone rang. "Here we go again," thought Christian, "Hello! Dogs Trust, Christian speaking, how can I help you?"

* * *

It was Monday morning in the Ellis household. "Sweetie" yelled Simone up the stairs, "hurry up. You need to walk River before school. I've taken on a longer shift today and we can't leave him for too long unless he's had a good walk. Actually, come home at lunchtime and spend half an hour with him. You could bring that boy if you like. What's his name again? Jenko, Jeckle... Jecko, that's it." She absentmindedly put the milk back in the fridge and stored the cereal packet back in the cupboard, mentally planning the rest of her day. "I'll be there now" shouted Simon, "I'm just doing my teeth." In an attempt to get her son to take his dental hygiene seriously, Simone had told Simon that, unless he brushed his teeth every morning straight after breakfast, they would wobble, then go black and fall out. Being Simon, he had assumed this would happen the second he finished eating and so would brush diligently for three minutes every morning. He timed it by listening to one of his favourite songs on his smart phone and tried to sing along at the same time. Once he'd finished, he would skip downstairs. He had every reason to skip these days, his dream of having his very own dog had actually come true, thanks to his mum. He took the steps two at a time and was greeted by a very waggy tailed River whose front paws were on the bottom step.

"Hello boy," said Simon, trying to avoid being whipped by his pet's rather thin, bony tail as he walked to the kitchen. It was, after all, just an extension of his spine and when it lashed his thigh, it really hurt. "Mum, it's an 'inset' day today. I couldn't tell you that from upstairs because my mouth was full of toothpaste." "Oh," said Simone, looking puzzled, "I thought that was next week. Oh well, you're old enough to look after yourself now although I would rather you had someone here with you. What's that boy, Jecko, doing today?" "Oh, nothing much, as usual," laughed Simon, "I'll text him now and see if he fancies coming on a dog walk. Is there anything in the fridge for lunch, Mum?" "Dunno sweetie, you'll have to have a rummage. I'll leave you a few quid to buy a sandwich in any case."

Simon was growing up and doing far better in school than his mum (or anyone else) could have imagined so Simone had taken on a slightly more interesting job as assistant manager at a local building firm. She kept their books and dealt with the customers; she enjoyed the new challenge and it brought in extra money which helped them to buy dog food and pay the odd vet's bill. Simon was her priority and River was his so she did all she could to make sure they were both well fed and happy.

'Ding dong, ding dong, ding dong' went the doorbell. "OK, OK" shouted Simone, "I'm coming, I'm coming." The front doorbell was quite piercing and when Simon was younger, he would put his hands over his ears and hide behind the sofa whenever it rang. Luckily, it didn't appear to have the same effect now he was older but she still ran to answer the door whenever she heard it, out of habit. Whoever was at the door clearly wanted it known that they were there. She could see a man through the frosted glass so she quickly put on the safety chain before opening the door a couple of inches. Since her ex-husband's mad girlfriend had started knocking at all hours of the day and night, demanding that Simone give her boyfriend a divorce, she had been very wary of opening the door to anyone she wasn't expecting. Eventually, she had taken pity on the poor, disillusioned girl with the streaky orange tan and straggly black hair extensions. "Scheherazade, sweetie, we've been divorced for over a year now, didn't he tell you?" She had long since stopped caring about Neil, where he was, what he was doing or whom he was dating. He had left her in the lurch, just when she'd needed his support and quite frankly, she would rather join a convent than consider getting back together with him. She needed a strong man in her life, or, nobody at all. Life with Simon and River was just lovely. Her son had matured into a really nice young man and having River in his life made him so happy, why would she want to ruin the whole thing by introducing a new fella into the equation?

Simon's dad clearly hadn't told his on-off girlfriend that he was footloose and fancy-free in case she demanded he put a ring on her finger and Scheherazade's face was a picture when she realised Neil had actually been divorced for over twelve months. She stormed off down the path, clippety-clopping in her cheap plastic high heels. She reached the end of the pathway and turned around, her eyes streaming with tears and shouted "Of course I knew. Do you think he didn't tell me? I just wanted to make sure you didn't think you were going to get back with him. He's mine now. Mine. You stay away, do you hear?" and off she wobbled, her 'Caribbean Bronze' tanning lotion running in rivulets down her cheeks. Simone almost felt sorry for her and found herself wondering, once again, whether any man was worth the heartache Neil had caused. Not just for her and for Simon but for his poor clingy, orange coloured girlfriend.

"Yes?" she said, peering past the safety chain, "how can I help you?" "Erm, well, it's like this..." stuttered Gareth, "I'm here to ask about..." "If you are selling anything, I'm sorry and I don't wish to appear rude but we don't want it, thank you," said Simone firmly and closed the door. The man knocked on the frosted glass and his muffled voice said "I'm sorry, I didn't want to upset you at all; I've come to ask you about your dog." Simone froze. What the heck did he mean? The dog was Simon's, who on earth was this person and how did he know they had a dog?

"Don't answer him Mum" said Simon who had come to see what all the commotion was about, "just ignore him, he'll go away." He had heard the man say he was enquiring about their dog and was more than a little worried that he was someone in authority who was going to say he couldn't, after all, keep River as a pet. This was inconceivable and he just wanted his mother to tell the man to go away. "Come on River, bark, for goodness sake" he hissed, "make some noise. We need this man to think you're really fierce so he'll go away and leave us alone." River, who had followed his beloved owner into the hallway, stood, wagging his tail and panting up at Simon. Greyhounds are not particularly noisy dogs; they get quite excited when people visit their kennels and on Race Days but on the whole, they are pretty quiet. Simone ushered Simon and a very excitable River into the kitchen and closed the door. "I have to go to work in a tick sweetie" she whispered, "but I don't want to leave you here alone with a strange man knocking on the door."

'Ding dong, ding dong, ding dong' rang the doorbell, 'Bang, bang, bang' went the door knocker. Simon, whose sensory problems were far less pronounced these days, put his hands over his ears and it was this that prompted Simone to march to the front door in anger. "Go away, just go away or I'll call the police. You're upsetting my son", she shouted through the glass. "You don't understand" shouted an increasingly desperate Gareth, "I think I recognise your dog. He was a racer and I'm sure I used to be one of his owners. I just wanted to know he was OK. Really."

Simon stared at his mum in horror. What now? What if the stranger had papers proving he owned River and wanted to take him away? He grabbed the dog lead and started to attach it to River's collar. He wasn't going to just stand there and let some man take away his beloved pet. Simone looked worried "Where are you going, sweetie?" "I don't know," he said angrily "but I'm certainly not just going to stand here and let some man I've never even met take River from me. Who is he? Where has he come from? If River was that important to him, why has he left it all this time before coming to find him?" "Calm down Simon," said his mum whose voice was wobbling now. She wished she had the answers and could tell her panicked son that everything would be OK but she wasn't too sure of things herself. Who was the man? Why had he come to look for River now and would he take him away if he could prove he owned him? She walked to the front door and made sure the door was locked, safety chain in place and went back into the kitchen to try and reason with Simon. She couldn't go off to work with him in this state. She was pretty sure the adoption papers would be proof enough but if this man had actual proof of ownership, could he refute the adoption and claim the dog as his own? She had no first clue as she'd never adopted an ex-racing greyhound before but she was not going anywhere until Simon had calmed down.

The back door was wide open and there was no sign of Simon or his precious hound. He'd taken the five pound note she had left on the table and thankfully, she noticed his mobile phone was gone from its usual place next to the microwave. River couldn't walk too quickly or for too long and she knew they wouldn't get too far away but Simon was upset and she didn't want him doing anything stupid. The dog was his life and she knew he would do anything to make sure nothing came between him and River. She reached for the phone to call the police but then, changed her mind and marched back out to the hallway. This had to be dealt with and it had to be dealt with right now.

Chapter Twenty One

Simone quietly removed the front door safety chain and then, flinging the door open wide, she shouted "NOW DO YOU SEE WHAT YOU'VE DONE? HE'S RUN AWAY AND I HAVE NO IDEA WHERE HE'LL GO AND…AND…" she sat down on the front step and burst into tears. Gareth looked startled and upset. "I'm really sorry, I have no idea what I've done but I'll try and explain if you'll let me." "There's no time for that," said Simone, wiping her eyes with her sleeve, "we have to find him. You've frightened him into thinking you're going to take River away and he's gone." Gareth was confused, he wasn't quite sure who had gone or who River was but he could sense he'd done enough damage so he said "Well, if you'll let me help, we could try and find him although I don't have much fuel in the car at the moment." "Aaarrrggghhhhh" screamed Simone, "you're not helping." She stood up, grabbed Lazarus's keys from the key hook, made sure her mobile phone was in her back pocket as usual, stepped outside the door and slammed it shut, barging past Gareth to get to the car.

"I could help you find him if you like" stumbled Gareth, knowing this was all his fault, "two pairs of eyes and all that..." "I don't know you" growled Simone as she opened the driver's door "but I'm warning you, if you annoy me, I will stop the car and put my hand on the horn until someone comes to help me, do you understand?" "Erm, yes," said a subdued Gareth, "absolutely."

He opened the passenger door, it was a tight squeeze as the car was so close to the low wall but he managed to slide in and put on his seat belt. Simone put Lazarus into reverse and Gareth heard a scraping noise as she reversed into the road rather too quickly. "Should I see you out?" he asked quietly. Simone didn't answer, she wasn't in the mood for pleasantries and she'd scraped the car too many times to be worried about today's damage. She racked her brains to think where Simon might have taken River and pointed the car towards the park. They got there in double quick time (Gareth hoped the rumours about there being no film in the local speed cameras were actually true) but there wasn't a single parking space to be had outside the park's main gate. Simone double parked and said brusquely "You stay there, you've done enough damage for one day" before running to the main gate, frantically scouring the grassy areas with her narrowed eyes. Nothing. No sign of them.

She couldn't imagine they would have got much further than the park and she needed to think hard about where else he might go. Somewhere he'd feel safe. Come on Simone, think, think!

She dashed back to the car, opened the passenger door and said "You drive, it'll be quicker. I could phone him but I can't do it while I'm driving." "But...but, I'm not insured to drive your car" protested Gareth, "what if we're stopped by the police?" "And what if I can't find my precious son and his precious dog?" she hissed, "please, just do it, just drive so I can think what to do next." He climbed into the driver's seat and, with some difficulty, pushed it backwards. Simone was only five foot two and anyone taller, trying to get their knees underneath the steering wheel, was in danger of causing themselves a mischief or at least stopping the blood from flowing through their legs. "Where now?" he asked, finally feeling as though she had dropped her guard a bit and was letting him help put right the problems he had caused. "Erm...erm, do a U-turn and just head back down this road while I make a phone call."

Gareth drove, being careful not to break the speed limit; he really couldn't afford to get into trouble for driving without insurance but he desperately wanted to help her. Despite her anger, she was obviously very worried about the missing person who, he had figured out, must be the boy he'd seen walking the dog across the pedestrian crossing the other day. He sensed there was no husband on the scene and he really was feeling awful to have caused this woman and her son such stress.

Simone seemed to be doing some kind of strange seated dance but then, he realised she was trying to get her mobile phone out from her back pocket. She managed to retrieve it and began dialling a number. "Jecko, Jecko, is that you? Simon's gone AWOL and he's taken River with him. Is he there with you?" Gareth could hear a mumbled voice on the other end of the phone but from its tone, he could tell it wasn't positive news. "Right, well, if he gets in touch, please let me know the second you hear from him. OK?" She hung up and sighed loudly. If he wasn't in the park and hadn't sought sanctuary at his friend's house, where on earth could Simon be? What's more, how on earth was he going to cope if River's legs gave way and he couldn't walk any further?

She had a brainwave. "Stop the car" she shouted, "turn around and head east out of the main town centre. I have an idea where he might be going although he'll be lucky if he gets anywhere near there." Gareth did as he was told and turned the car around. They started driving due east, the housing estates fading away behind them and eventually, they found themselves driving Lazarus along a rather pot-hole riddled country road. "Where are we going?" ventured Gareth, fully prepared to have his head snapped off again. "We adopted River from the Dogs Trust," said Simone, "I wonder whether he would take him back there? It's just a hunch but worth a try." They drove in silence, Gareth not daring to speak or try and explain anything. He would wait until she had calmed down a bit more. He realised he didn't even know this woman's name but he did know her son was called Simon, he had a friend called Jecko and for some reason, she thought the dog's name was River.

Gareth slammed his foot on the brake and shouted "Look, look. There they are!" Simone, whose hair had flung itself over her eyes when Gareth had braked, peered through her fringe, trying to see what he was looking at. Sure enough, it was a teenage boy and a dog.

They were walking very slowly and the dog's back legs kept buckling beneath him. Simone knew her son would never hurt River so he must be desperate to keep him walking until they reached the Dogs Trust.

Simon kept stopping and appeared to be talking to the dog. Simone didn't want to scare him into trying to run, River was in no fit state to run anywhere and the long walk had not helped his legs. It had taken them about fifteen minutes of driving to find them, they had walked a long way in that time so she could only imagine they'd set off at a bit of a lick in order to reach the road they were on.

Gareth put the car into first gear and very slowly parked close to the grass verge. It was a quiet road but he put the hazard lights on as a precaution; he wanted to make sure any other motorists could see the car. Simone got out and started walking quickly, she broke into a trot and eventually, she caught up with Simon who was crying. "Simon, sweetie, come on now, you have to stop trying to walk him so quickly. His legs won't take it, you know that." River, recognising Simone's voice, wagged his tail. She melted. The poor dog was in a terrible state, limping along because Simon wanted him to keep up. For the first time ever, she really saw what Simon saw in this poor, broken down dog. Through no fault of his own, he was permanently injured and although he didn't know it, it was humans who had caused his difficulties. Through his tears, Simon gulped "But that man's going to take him, you heard him, he said he used to own River so he must have some sort of right over him. I can't let him go Mum, I don't know

what would happen to him. I love him so much."
Simone started crying too, she had never heard such an
impassioned speech from her son, he usually kept his
emotions under wraps and it was only the odd brief
hug or shoulder squeeze which told her how much her
son cared for her.

She said "Don't you worry about the man. We've been
driving together for a while and he seems OK. If I'd
thought he was dodgy in any way, I wouldn't even have
let him into the car. Come on, let's go home, have a cup
of tea and hear him out. I won't let him take River,
I promise." She held up her right hand with its little
finger crooked "Pinky promise?" He smiled and wiped
away his tears. "Muuuuum, I don't do Pinky promise
now, I'm a teenager, remember?" She so wanted to hug
him but she knew it would make things worse. He
would try and avoid being hugged and she would be
upset so she just patted him on the shoulder and took
River's lead. "Come on boy, let's go home," she said
quietly. River wobbled, his back legs were going to give
up the ghost unless she put him into the car quickly.

Simone's phone rang, she gave Simon the dog lead and
mouthed "Put him on the back seat" before saying "Hi
Jecko, thanks for calling back. Yes, we've found him.
It's a long story, I'll get him to ring you later. Thanks
again, bye bye." She walked slowly back towards the
car, hoping River was going to be OK after his ordeal
and then, a very strange and unexpected thing happened.

Chapter Twenty-Two

River spotted Gareth standing beside the driver's door and, to Simon's surprise (and Simone's astonishment) he tried to walk a little faster. He started wagging his tail and by the time he was up close, he seemed very excited indeed. "Hello boy" said Gareth, as he stroked his head, "it's good to see you again." River nuzzled Gareth's thigh, it was his way of showing affection and it brought a lump to Gareth's throat to see poor Hero in such a state. He had been a fine racer, a famous champion and now, he found it difficult to walk any distance at all.

Simone watched the unexpected reunion from a distance. It was clear the dog recognised the man (she really must find out his name) so she needed to know exactly who he was and what his connection was to River before contacting the Dogs Trust to speak to Christian. She might need his help in proving they'd officially adopted the dog but she was prepared to hear the man out first. She got back to the car and said "Well, he obviously recognises you, I've never seen him react like that before. I've just realised I don't know your name; mine's Simone Ellis and my son's name is Simon. You've met River so why don't we all go back to our house, put the kettle on and you can tell us how you found us and what you want." She didn't sound angry but Gareth sensed she was on the defensive so he nodded and got into the passenger seat. There was no point in trying to explain things now, he would wait until he could speak to them both face to face. "I'm Gareth, Gareth Evans and yes, let's go back to yours and I'll try and explain everything to you there."

They drove in silence and as they approached number seven, Simone parked the car on the road, close to the kerb just outside the house. She knew getting River out of the car would be difficult and there simply wasn't room in the narrow driveway. They all got out and Gareth helped Simon to manoeuvre River's legs so they could lift him out. He was panting, dogs sometimes pant when they're stressed so Gareth said "Come on butty, that's the way, we'll have you inside in no time." River ground to a halt and his legs started shaking; he simply couldn't walk the few steps to the front door so Gareth gently scooped him up in his arms and carried him to the house. Simon began to soften towards him, he obviously cared about River and wanted to help so maybe he wasn't so bad after all.

Simone was exhausted but she opened the front door and asked Gareth and Simon to take River to the front room, where his bed lay next to the television. She forced her tired legs to walk the few extra steps to the kitchen, filled the kettle, hit the 'On' switch and found some biscuits in a cupboard. She placed two cups of tea, a small jug of milk, the sugar bowl, a plate of biscuits and a glass of orange squash onto an old tea tray and slowly walked to the lounge, nudging the door open with her foot. Simon was sitting on the floor with River's head in his lap, he was stroking the dog's head and whenever he stopped, River would paw at him to make him start again. Greyhounds are quiet dogs but they do have a way of letting you know what they want.

Gareth was still standing up and was talking to someone on his mobile and smiling broadly. "Really? That's great news, couldn't have come at a better time. Thank you. I have to go now but thank you very much." He put his phone away and said "Sorry, just someone ringing with some news about a job interview I had last week. I start next month." He noticed Simone's rather tired expression and said "Sorry, you don't really care about that do you?"

Simone said stiffly "Please, do sit down" and nodded towards an old armchair which had seen better days, "Would you like black or white tea? Do you take sugar?" She felt a little frustrated. There she was, trying hard to make ends meet and he had just been told he had a new job to look forward to. Gareth, sensing her mood, thought it best to just keep quiet about the new job. She couldn't possibly know he'd been out of work for months on end after he'd left his job. Or that, when he had found freelance work, the money sometimes didn't even cover his monthly bills. He sat in the tatty old chair, he could feel the springs coming through the base; it really wasn't very comfortable. He thought he might buy them a new one when his first pay cheque came through, to say 'sorry' for today.

"So, what is your connection to our dog?" asked Simone, pouring herself a strong cup of black tea "and before you start, I just want you to know that he is now Simon's pet and he's going nowhere, is that understood?" She handed Gareth the plate of biscuits, he shook his head "No thanks, not for me" and then began his explanation of how he had come to knock on their door that afternoon.

"As I told you, my name is Gareth Evans, I'm originally from Wales but I moved here about ten years ago, with my work. It was a good job and I managed to save a few quid each month. One of my colleagues had been on a night out to the local dog track and he suggested a few of us buy our own racer. We all chipped in equal amounts and did some research about how to buy a greyhound. We eventually chose one from a very good litter, both his parents had been champions in their day so we appointed a well-respected trainer and raced the dog for a few years until he was injured in a terrible collision at the track." Simone dunked a biscuit in her tea, her facial expression giving nothing away. She just wanted to hear his story, from start to finish, before she asked him to leave and never come back.

Gareth took a sip of tea and continued "Unfortunately the other owners decided that, because we would no longer be winning any prize money, they didn't want to have to pay for his treatment or his upkeep and because I couldn't afford to do it on my own, I had to go along with the plan of lying low until people stopped ringing us. We just kept on passing the buck to one another but eventually, the track, the kennels and everyone just stopped calling, which is exactly what we wanted to happen."

Simone finally spoke "That was a bit cowardly if you don't mind my saying. This poor dog won you thousands of pounds and you just walked away from him the minute something went wrong." Her cold tone made Gareth feel even worse about himself than he had when he'd first seen Hero hobbling towards the car earlier that day. "I know, I know and I hate myself for being such a wimp. We had heard that the Retired Greyhound Trust might step in and pay for his food and upkeep so we just crossed our fingers that this was true and kept shtum about the whole thing." He looked across at Hero who wagged his tail at him, just to make him feel even worse. "I did set up a second e-mail account and sent a few quid via their website but of course, I don't know whether it went to help him or just went into the general pot. I tried to track him down recently but the people at one of the local shelters sounded very suspicious and I thought I might be hauled up in front of a judge or something so I just hung up." He was hanging his head in shame now, what on earth must this woman and her son think of him? "I would happily have adopted him but the others sort of steamrollered me and in any case, my landlord won't allow pets..." Gareth's voice trailed off and he stared down at his teacup.

Simone had listened intently to Gareth's story and now, it was her turn to speak. "So, you're saying you used to actually own this dog as part of some sort of syndicate?" "Yes," said Gareth, "there were six of us in total." He didn't want to upset her or her son any more than he had already, so he kept his answers short and to the point. "What do you think about this sweetie?" she asked Simon, worried that the stress of this man ciaiming to have owned her son's pet would cause some kind of regression. He had been doing so brilliantly and was so happy with his dog, she couldn't bear it if anything caused him to take a turn backwards.

"Well," said Simon slowly, "River obviously knows him and doesn't seem worried or unhappy that he's here so I supposed he must like him or at the very least, he's not scared of him." He stroked River's head and the dog gave a wag; he felt safe and secure with Simon, they had hit it off so quickly and were a very close partnership now. Simone asked, "So what happened next?"

"He was a champion, he was the best there was. He never lost a race" Gareth reminisced, "There wasn't anyone who hadn't heard of Handsome Hero." River pricked up his ears and Simon exclaimed "Handsome Hero? Was that his racing name?" "Yes", said Gareth, "but we called him 'Hero' for short. Look at his ears, I think he remembers his old name. Out of interest, why do you call him 'River'?" he asked, bravely helping himself to a biscuit. Simone said "Well, it seems he escaped from wherever he was kennelled and fell into the river. He was rescued by some bloke who was fishing and an ambulance man. They called the Dogs Trust who took him to a vet. He was in a bit of a state, having fought the river currents for some time. He almost went over the weir but they managed to fish him out just in time. The vet said he had old racing injuries in his back legs and managed to operate and put pins in or something but because of where he'd been found, they nicknamed him 'River' and it sort of stuck."

"Do you mind if I call him by his old name, to see his reaction?" asked Gareth. Simone looked at Simon who shrugged and said "OK"; now he knew the man wasn't going to try and take him away, he was much more relaxed although he wasn't sure about a different name. He liked things to stay the same, it made him feel secure and less anxious. "Hero?" called Gareth, "Hello Hero, hello boy, how are you?" Hero pricked up his ears even higher and thumped his tail on the bed. Simon was amazed, he'd been calling his dog 'River' for months but he did appear to remember his old racing name. Given the terrible journey he'd been on, he really was quite a hero and he mulled the name over in his brain, wondering whether he could get used to it too.

Gareth gave a wry smile and said "If you knew the hours I'd spent worrying about him and wondering where he was, you might understand that I just had to find out whether he had survived his accident at the track and maybe found a good home. I can see I had absolutely nothing to worry about, you clearly love him and he seems very happy indeed. Don't you boy?" He put down his cup of tea and knelt by the dog's bed. Hero licked his hand and looked up at him with big brown eyes. "They are so forgiving aren't they?" mused Gareth, "I was very angry with the other owners; they wouldn't listen to me. All I wanted was for us all to chip in a few quid every month, to pay for his food and kennel fees but they said 'No' and not one of them would help me out. I hated going into work after that, hated even having to be in the same building as them all. Eventually, when everything had died down and we stopped worrying about them contacting us, I left my job." He stroked Hero's head as he spoke, "in fact, I had a bit of a breakdown over it all."

Simone put her empty cup on the coffee table and looked across at Simon who gave her a small smile. "So," she asked Gareth, "if things had been different, you might have adopted River...erm, Hero yourself?" "Oh yes," said Gareth, "absolutely. If my landlord had been OK about pets, I would have had him like a shot. I even lost my girlfriend over it all, the whole thing was a bit of a black time in my life really." "I'm sorry to hear that," said Simone, thinking she had maybe been a bit hasty in condemning him before hearing his side of the story. Hero had placed his head in Gareth's lap now so Simone said "Sweetie, why don't you go and give Jecko a ring? He was a bit worried about you, I told him you'd explain everything when you called." Simon could see Hero was comfortable and relaxed so he got up, stretched his legs and said "OK Mum. What's for tea?" She grimaced; she hadn't even thought about tea.

After Simon had left the room, his mum closed the door quietly and said "Simon is autistic and you turning up out of the blue and rattling him like that really wasn't fair. I know you didn't know about the autism but I'm just telling you so you're more aware. He likes routine, he likes to know where he's at. River, I mean Hero, is exercised twice a day, come hell or high water. He is fed at the same times each day and he is also in a very good routine. I understand that you used to be a part of his life but he's Simon's pride and joy so I would be grateful if you would just say goodbye and leave quietly."

Gareth looked down at Hero sadly. "If things had been different, butty," he said in his sing-song Rhondda accent, "you might still be mine but I can see how happy you are here so I'll just get off and I won't bother you again." Hero's tail thumped up and down, he was enjoying all the attention and Simone noticed Gareth tickling behind his ears, just as Simon had the very first time he visited the Dogs Trust. This told her Gareth knew the dog well and she marvelled at how the dog had warmed to him so quickly, despite not having seen his former co-owner for years. She was beginning to realise that greyhounds, despite the hand dealt to them by the human race on occasion, were the most forgiving of creatures and she even felt slightly sorry for Gareth, having heard his story properly from start to finish. She wondered whether Simon would cope with him visiting Hero from time to time and while she collected up the cups and plate, she decided she would ask him later on. Now then, what the heck was she going to give Simon for his tea?

Chapter Twenty Three

"Mum, Jecko's here!" Simon's head popped around the lounge door just as Gareth was standing up to leave. "We're starving, is there anything to eat?" Simone groaned, it was that time again. She looked up to heaven and explained to Gareth, "I hate cooking. I'm quite good at some things but wielding a spatula is very definitely not one of them." "Alright, Mrs Ellis? Don't worry about food or nuffink, I can always get some chips from the chippy later on. I'm glad River's back though." "Hero" interjected Simon, "his real name's Hero and I think he's a real Hero so I've decided to change it back. If that's OK Mum?" She smiled across at her happy, smiling son and said "He's your dog sweetie, you can call him whatever you like."

Gareth took a deep breath and said "Listen, you lot don't know me from Adam but I feel I've caused you all a lot of trouble today. If you'll let me, I'd like to take you to the pub up the road. It's dog-friendly so we can take Hero in the car and put him on his bed in their garden, he's not up to doing much more walking today, is he? They do great pizzas." He smiled at the boys who both looked at each other, licking their lips. "Pizza! Yay!" shouted Simon and Hero wagged his tail to hear his favourite person so excited.

"Well…" said Simone. "Oh Mum, pretty please, can we go for pizza?" begged Simon. "I ain't had nuffink to eat since breakfast" said Jecko, rubbing his stomach in glee. "OK then" she laughed, "let's go for pizza. Thank you very much, it's very kind of you" she said to Gareth "but I thought you were broke after you left your job." "I've been freelancing for some time but that phone call was a very happy bolt from the blue. I start my new, full-time job next month. I felt it was about time I got back into a routine and I'm pretty sure I can run to pizza for four today." "By the way," asked Simone, picking up her keys and her handbag, "how did you find us? How did you know Hero lived here with us?" "I didn't," said Gareth, holding the door for her, "I happened to be driving a different way home last week and saw Simon and his friend with Hero. They were crossing the road and I couldn't believe my eyes so I followed them and saw Simon walk Hero up your path. It was a big decision to come knocking at your door I can tell you."

Simone walked down the rather crooked pathway, towards the car. "We'll need to put Hero in the back seat again, I'll open the door and you can bring him out. The boys can walk, it's not far." Gareth coaxed Hero off his bed and attached his lead to his special wide leather greyhound collar. "Come on boy, sorry to disturb you but we're off to the pub now and you're coming too." Hero took a few steps, the rest seemed to have done him good and he walked gingerly by himself to the car. Simone and Gareth helped him up onto the back seat and covered his damaged legs with a tartan blanket. They put his bed in the boot, for him to lie on in the Beer Garden of the Four Ferrets pub. Simone shouted to Simon and Jecko, who were walking ahead, chatting happily. "Make sure you get us a nice table in the shade, it's too hot for River, erm, Hero to be in the sun." They gave the OK sign with their hands and carried on walking and chatting about the day's events. They were happy to go on ahead and in any case, they sensed the grown-ups had more talking to do.

Simone put the key in the ignition and then, paused what she was doing, her hand still on the keys. "If someone had told me my Simon would, one day, have a best friend and his very own dog, I would never have believed them." "Well," said Gareth, gently, knowing it was a special moment for her, "he looks very happy and it's no more than he deserves. He's a fine boy and a real credit to you." She blushed. "Do you think so?" "Yes I do," he said "my cousin has a boy with autism so I do know how difficult the whole social thing can be. My nephew is doing quite well but your son is doing brilliantly. It must be wonderful to see him so happy."

They set off for the pub, Simone driving very slowly so Hero wouldn't be forced to move at all. "So, what happened to your girlfriend then?" she ventured, looking straight ahead as if she wasn't really that interested. "Erm, my...erm, girlfriend..." he stammered, feeling a little nervous "well, when Hero was injured, she decided she didn't love me any more. To be honest, I'm not sure it was love in the first place. She gave me a right old earful about how 'stewpid' I was and what a 'stewpid' dog Hero had been for getting himself injured and then, she left, taking everything I'd ever bought her." Simone smiled at the windscreen, "She sounds charming." Gareth looked out through his side of the windscreen and said "She was a user. She fell in love with my wallet when Hero was winning race after race. It was nothing to do with me being me, it was more about the kudos, the fame, the champagne and the high life. Oh, and the handbags. She did like a nice designer handbag, did Donna."

"Handbags are nothing more than slightly posher versions of plastic carrier bags in my world" laughed Simone, "I have one black one, one brown one and one white one. I use them for transporting my phone, my purse, my keys and my lipstick but other than that, they are of no use to me. Same with clothes and shoes. I only wear them so people don't point and laugh at me in public." Gareth laughed out loud and said "We have a lot in common in that case. It never did sit well with me really, making lots of money from dog racing. The others loved the whole experience but I couldn't help feeling something might happen to Hero one day and, I was right, it did and then, the others just walked away from him." "Are you in touch with them at all?" asked Simone. "No," said Gareth, "they really are not my kind of people. They never were." They stopped at the traffic lights. Gareth turned around to stroke Hero "You OK boy?" Simone looked across at him and thought to herself 'Y'know what? He really is quite nice'.

The lights changed to green and Simone drew away slowly, the pub was in sight and the two boys were jumping up and down, pretending to hitch a lift from them. She turned Lazarus into the car park, it was nice and wide so there was no danger of her scratching the back of the car. She put on the handbrake and drew in a breath. "If you're not doing anything next weekend, would you like to come and see us? We could maybe go to the park, take a picnic? If Hero isn't able to walk any better, I'll take him to the vet but we could always drive him there. The boys could always walk to the park and I could....sorry, I'm rambling now. What I mean is, would you like to?"

Gareth smiled across at Simone and said "Do you know what? I think I'd like that very much."

Author biography

Fiona Bennett was born in Cardiff and for most of her professional life has worked as a pianist, singer, composer, songwriter and bandleader. This year (2016) Fiona's two classical albums, 'A Country Suite' and 'The New Lady Radnor Suite' were voted into the Classic FM 'Hall of Fame' Top 300 chart.

Fiona suffers with allergies and asthma but was amazed to find greyhounds didn't trigger her symptoms at all. She adopted Saracen (an ex-racer who had been thrown out onto the streets) from Dogs Trust in Newbury in 1997 and her love of this gentle breed prompted her to adopt her current three 'girls' from the Oxford branch of the Retired Greyhound Trust.

She adopted Amber as a companion for her younger son, Zachary, when his elder brother, Dominic, went to boarding school. He had always been frightened of dogs but, since adopting Amber, Rosie and Cleopatra, he now wants to 'chat' to every dog he meets!

Fiona's story about Simon (a boy with autism) and Hero (a discarded champion racer) draws on her own experience of autism and also her knowledge of adopting ex-racing greyhounds. The story was partly written to raise awareness of the plight of greyhounds once their racing careers have ended, but also to educate those reading the book about the difficulties of living with autism.

Fiona is a supporter of the Retired Greyhound Trust and half the proceeds of this book will go towards helping them find 'furever' homes for as many ex-racers as possible.

Fiona lives in Berkshire and recently married her old Guildhall School of Music and Drama pal, John Heritage.

www.fionabennettmusic.co.uk